T0054424

THE PUNISHER

STAN A. COWIE

THE PUNISHER

iUniverse books may be ordered through booksellers or by contacting:

iUniverse
1663 Liberty Drive
Bloomington, IN 47403
www.iuniverse.com
1-800-Authors (1-800-288-4677)

ISBN: 978-1-4917-4068-2 (sc)
ISBN: 978-1-4917-4067-5 (e)

Library of Congress Control Number: 2014913504

Printed in the United States of America.

iUniverse rev. date: 7/28/2014

ACKNOWLEDGEMENTS

Thanks to the RAF Regiment for sending me on two one-year tours in the Gulf of Aden, Yemen, Kenya and Tanzania. Without the knowledge I gained on those tours this book wouldn't have been possible.

My lovely wife Louella, always there with the encouragement, always!

The I Universe staff that made this all happen and let me enjoy yet another completed work.

Thank you Chris Gillet for great editing, you made life easy for me. We'll do it again.

My son James, thanks for all the info on the latest technology available, it's mind-boggling, thanks Jim.

Most of all thank you to Lt Colonel USAR (Ret.) Robert K Brown, publisher of Soldier of Fortune magazine and author of 'I Am Soldier of Fortune' and 'Dancing with Devils', for all the info I could glean from his writing. Thanks!

CHAPTER 1

THE INTENSITY OF THE DESERT HEAT WAS MORE THAN most humans would be able to tolerate, but the prone figure remained buried in the sand. Nothing showed but his eyes, as they peered from their shaded slits. The winds of the night before had washed over everything. Not a track was to be seen, nothing out of place for twenty miles in any direction.

And he watched the village below. Eight hundred yards out, on a one-in-four decline. Nothing moved, nothing lived. What had once been a thriving community now lay in ruins. A shell of its past, the tower of the mosque still stood, barely. The school, the only place of education for miles around, normally filled with children, burned. Bodies lay scattered where they had fallen, men, women and children. The old Sheik's home, or palace, as he liked to think of it; a modest dwelling where heads of the village used to enjoy a pipe, and sit and suck the smoke from the dried cinnamon mixed with Turkish tobacco through the cool water of their crystal bowls. The dogs that warned the village of approaching friends or foe, lay dead. Camels, donkeys, nothing lived, only the scavengers of the desert. As they struggled to

1

rise, their bellies filled with putrid flesh. The orchards and date palms were devastated.

One week ago this village had been a thriving community. The gateway to the sand sea. Camel trains had resupplied, stocked and traded before they made the return trip across the sand seas for the precious salt and dry goods they would return with. Tourists rarely visited this location, nothing for them to take home; there were no trinkets or memorabilia. Now, nothing but smoldering ruins. And the silence that only the desert could give.

This was broken by the distant thump of the rotors from the three gunships as they came from out of the dying sun, circling the village in a wide arc and closing in. One at a time they came to light in front of the mosque remains, circling and dropping on their skids. There they sat, the sand swirling in great clouds, no more than 20 yards from the shattered door of the mosque. The rotors started their wind down. And slowly the dusty sand settled, and once again silence prevailed.

A door slid open, simultaneously the figure buried in the sand rolled over onto his back, sand slid from the poncho that had covered him. Without taking his eyes from the scene below, he unzipped a holdall and started to assemble the weapon he had carried in the day before. Barely a pint was left in the two gallon jug of tepid water that was buried in the sand, no more than a foot from his location. A small clear tube fed from the jug to his mouth. He sucked it dry and spat the tube out, now giving his full attention to the weapon in front of him.

A 50-caliber BMG M82A1, that was its technical tag, better known to the man in the field as the Beretta 50, and a 5-clip box mag holding hand-loaded projectiles. Short tripod, 29" barrel topped with a Swarovski 12 x 50 mil-dot and built-in range finder. Each piece removed from a sealed compartment in the holdall.

Now it sat on its short-legged tripod, trained on the scene below, there wasn't a long range shooter that wouldn't bleed, just to lay behind this weapon and squeeze off a shot. At one mile out this weapon would devastate a human body. And now it was a tool in the hands of a craftsman. The Swarovski was known for its ability to suck up the last rays of light and bring them back to life. Today it would be used and returned to its home in Tel Aviv. A certain police armorer would clean it and return it to its own holdall. The rightful owner would never know it had left its home.

The marksman slid his eye over the aperture and it came to life. The first member from the open door was in full Arab dress carrying the working man's AK47. He immediately ran to the side door and slid it open and waited. Six men alighted from the other choppers, all carrying the same armament and gathered around the largest of the three birds. A dark form appeared from this machine and descended to the hard-packed sand, the only one wearing dark headgear but with his back to the marksman, definitely taller than the rest, by at least three inches. He turned and looked right in to the mil-dots. The Hawk - the goatee, the patch over his right eye, there was no mistaking him from the picture in the patch pocket of his combat pants. The target!

"Must be a bitch being right handed and no right eye," he thought.

"Don't worry bud, all the lights will be out soon, then we can both go home, you to Paradise and all those damned virgins. Me! To the fishing in Kinbasket Lake."

And he squeezed the trigger. The Hawk's throat exploded as the expanded 50-caliber projectile tore through it, ripping out his Adam's apple and spinal cord, barely leaving enough sinew and skin to stop his head from separating from his body. The closest guard, sprayed with blood and shards of bone embedded in his face and eyes, dropped his weapon and clawed at his face screaming in pain and fear. When the butt plate hit the hard-packed dirt, the breach slid and caught a round sending it screaming off the stone wall of the mosque, a good sign of worn out equipment and lack of maintenance.

The choppers banged and spluttered as they were forced into an early pre-start. Throttles were wrenched open trying for an immediate lift off, bodies scrambled and threw themselves on the decks as the birds lifted. Bullets sprayed through the open hatches at an invisible target. As the larger of the three birds rose, it twisted and raised its tail, exposing its underbelly. A 50-caliber projectile tore into its fuel cell, erupting into a fireball.

Jagged shards of metal sliced into the other birds, almost bringing them down as they deployed and went swooping low behind large dunes and weaving an escape route. The diminishing sound of the rotors told they were heading for faraway places.

"Well the pearly gates of Islam would be busy this fine sunset," he mumbled.

By the time silence had returned to the sand seas the

Beretta 50 was stripped and returned to its holdall, every piece carefully placed in its compartment and zipped away with the overlapping velcro tabs firmly closed.

A thin nylon line attached to his combat boot was yanked tight, causing a small rooster-tail of sand, exposing the corner of a lightweight tarp. This was laboriously pulled back exposing another.

The second was split in the middle and overlapped, keeping all the sand out. These were also flipped open exposing an 800 Polaris ATV modified for the US Army, with larger fuel cells and storage pods. For those who don't know, it is a four-wheel drive motorcycle that will climb the side of a house and reach 100 kilometres an hour, if you can hold on to it. You can sink it in mud and it will just climb out, a hunter's dream, a bird watcher's nightmare. This evening it would transport the shooter back to civilisation, it was fired up and it spun its way out of its canvas-shrouded pit and sat there idling.

The tarps were folded back down the pit, empty water jug went after it, then it was back-filled, all traces of the sniper's existence. Empty cases were in his pocket, the sand smoothed over. From one of the pods on the ATV a Claymore mine was extracted and primed, then buried in the sand with the corner of an Egyptian five pound note sticking out.

"Get one, get both!"

He sometimes thought he had a creative streak.

"This could remain for a year and never be discovered, but I'll lay odds there will be a sweep through here by first light."

With a final glance over the area, the ATV was

mounted and the throttle pinned, sending a rooster-tail of sand high into the air as it shot forward into the diminishing light.

As much mileage would be obtained before full dark, the winds would arise and start their never-ending task of moving the sand. Every morning was a new picture in the sand seas.

A red dot on the green glowing screen of the GPS showed the route to the only pre-planned fuel dump. Deployment might be necessary and extra fuel crucial, there was no faster way to cross the sand seas. The machine maintained its speed, till full dark. A high spot was reached and the engine cut; the only sound was the rising wind and the tiny pinging and cracking of the cooling engine. Night vision goggles were brought to bear.

The terrain behind was scanned for any pursuit, in front for any obstacles. The ground cover started to change, rock started to appear. Wadis became more frequent and sand became gravel.

The silence prevailed. This was good, no birds in the air.

The return of the choppers had been an ongoing threat, but not after dark. They wouldn't have the balls for that.

Regardless of whether Allah offered a better life in the next world, they were not all in a hurry to leave this one. Him neither! Bread and goats cheese with tepid water to wash it down were taken.

Then he moved off the ridge. The GPS was indicating he was close. The machine dipped down into a shallow wadi and the crack with the jerry can was located. You could smell it before you saw it.

Evaporation in this climate always took its toll. Refuelling was carried out and the rest tipped into the sand.

The machine left the wadi and with lights on, resumed its route. This would last for approximately half an hour. Then the half-moon would be up and a million stars would show the way. The desert would return to light again. Headlights would not be required.

Most successful raids in the desert were pre-dawn. The Legion and Le Para spent a lot of years in the sand learning this. The LRDG later to become the SAS learned from them. The Brits hated to admit they could learn anything from the French, and the good old US of A learned from them all. Thus the success of the Navy Seals and special forces, a true professional soldier speaks many tongues and walks many lands. Usually scorned for his victories and sneered at for his losses. They have no delusions of grandeur, it's services rendered for a price paid. This is what he was - a mercenary.

The quad (ATV) dipped down and started a descent to a small silver line that was the unpaved road to Attiaf. It took 15 minutes to reach through the increased rock and shale. The ATV fish-tailed onto this trail, as that was all it was, then straightened out. The throttle pinned to the max and it shot forward.

Attiaf should be reached before daylight. It took an hour and a half until the last rise was crossed and the machine was allowed to coast down the grade towards the village of Attiaf. Half a mile before the village he veered off and dropped into a dry wash and the engine was cut. The first house on the outside of the village looked like a small square box. One door, two windows, this was the home of Yasat a friendly, supposed to be! He removed his Glock from its shoulder holster, slid the action, saw the brass, let it slide back and held it down his leg, you just never know, and raised his hand to knock when the door was jerked open, the camel-hide hinges squealing in protest.

"Hi bud, a bit late aren't you?."

"Yo Sarge, the traffic was atrocious."

He grabbed his hand and started pumping it, dragging him inside and closing the door with his butt.

"Hope you had fun with the US Army toys."

"That I did. That I did, Sarge!"

"Where the hell is it then?"

"At the bottom of the wash."

"Not all beat up is it? Like, full of fucking bullet holes."

"Shit man, what do you think I do?"

"I don't want to know. Don't even hint."

"Nothing! OK? Am I paid?"

"Same as before, best money you ever had, and you'll see that the holdall catches its flight AOK?"

"You got it man, it's done."

"Better get your ass in gear, your ride will be here pronto."

He stripped off his combat gear and climbed into his robes. The combat equipment was already smoking on the small cook fire. Boots traded for sandals after his feet got a good dusting down.

His money belt held a small amount of currency and the little bag over his shoulder carried a small amount of food and tied to that was a prayer mat. He bowed his head in shame, Bedouins were a proud people, but only as camel jockeys. Riding on a bus was not part of the deal, so he bowed his head and hid his face in shame.

"Man you are good, you even smell of camel. Got to go bud! If you need my services again, just let me know."

"Thanks Sarge."

And he was gone. It took ten minutes and he could hear the ATV come to life and scramble up the opposite side, heading on its way to the US Air base. At the same time he heard the rickety bus come clattering down the single lane alley.

It shuddered to a stop beside him. He climbed on board and dropped the appropriate coins in his tray and mumbled Jeddah and shuffled off back among the chicken crates and dried goods, to find a seat and fake going to sleep. He left the bus on the outskirts of Jeddah and walked till he caught a cab and took it to within 100 yards of the Cleopatra Hotel.

After the cabbie had gone he just sat on the curb with all the other vagrants. He gave it 15 and before someone started to converse, he got up and left, walking to the hotel. It had the same name as the smokes in Cairo.

He had left a room there four days ago, with a small suitcase and a change of clothes, some paperwork stating he was a purchaser of leather goods for a London distributor.

CHAPTER 2

HE HADN'T HAD ANY LUCK IN JEDDAH AND WAS RETURNING to Cairo, and that was apparent, as he had two slips in his battered briefcase, stating they didn't want to do business at this time, maybe in the future. He also had a sizeable order from Yehia Massoud Leather and Fine Goods on Chawarby Street, Cairo.

After a lukewarm shower, the first in four days, he checked out, and with the help of a Mazda cab that shouldn't have been allowed on the fucking road, he made his flight from Jeddah to Cairo; that's where all the paper came into play. The customs people in Saudi were not nice people, they read everything you showed them and anything they found, they then discussed it with their associate and scowl at you like you shouldn't be even riding on one of their planes.

Wog cabbies he'd always liked. They kind of gave him that feeling he was on the edge, like a rollercoaster that's not working right. Now the cabbies in Jeddah were slow stuff compared to Cairo. It's like all the cabbies in Cairo were out of work NASCAR drivers or just too dangerous to qualify. The cabbie came to greet you and you made a deal before you got in the cab. Great, you got a good price.

Then he scooped up your luggage and disappeared into the throng that is Cairo, leaving the heaviest piece for you, of course! It's true they were crazy drivers, not stupid. Then you got to see the ride you thought you did so well bartering for. Man if there was a piece of metal not dinted, it had got to be the roof. What you would likely get was a vintage Mercedes that had seen one of those golf ball hailstorms they always brag about in Montana or worse Canada! Now this guy left the airport like the Gates of Islam were giving free tours.

The horn was on a non-stop blare, they taped them to the gear shift so it didn't interfere with their driving. There were people diving in all directions.

He looked over the cabbie's shoulder at the dash gauges, just out of curiosity, nothing worked, just a black hole with wires hanging out of it. You didn't know how much fuel he had, or how fast you were travelling. But it was fast! Oh, another thing in Cairo, traffic lights just didn't have the same interest to a Cairo driver as anywhere else in the world, you see, if you stayed close enough together you could get through amber, and red and likely the three or four cars behind you could as well.

The Cleopatra Hotel gave him his first good meal and his second shower, this one was hot. And he was on his way to London. Only now did he count himself out of the woods, unless the pricks had a bomb on the plane. He had no hassle at the airport, his Arabic was pretty good in two or three dialects.

His suit was shabby and dirty and he hadn't shaved in five days, like the sarge said, he smelled of camel. He smoked Cleo, the main brand in Cairo, he was one of the guys, and with a Brit passport he had it made, big time. It was a poor man's dream in Cairo to own a Brit passport. He wondered if the old Sheik was happy with his work. He had a premonition this was going to happen and he was to avenge the village by termination of the Hawk. This to him was worth ten big ones plus expenses, US deposited in a bank in Cyprus. They got the money, he got the Visa.

Knocks the shit out of the Canadian Tax system, as he had no holdings in Canada as far as they knew. He use the card and Cyprus paid the bills. He kept a low profile in Canada, living just above the poverty line. Things had been a bit slow lately, what with 9-11 and all this terrorist stuff going down. It made it a little hard leaving the country. Your average tourist didn't go to Afghanistan or Lebanon without drawing a little attention to themselves.

Feast or famine would be the way to describe his income. He led a modest lifestyle living approximately 200km from a small town, nestled in the foothills of the Rocky Mountains. He fished, hunted, usually by himself or with the dog. That is breaking the rules a bit but he liked the hunt as much as his owner did. They hunted for the meat and the sport. And he was still spending the Sheik's money in his head when the 747 touched down in the rain at Gatwick.

He had to make a couple of calls. To the company he got his order from in Cairo, they were big suppliers and very respected in this field, jackets, coats, bags, all leather - the best. This was a place you didn't shop unless you wanted to drop your whole check in one place. He was definitely outclassed but knew the product, just had a feel for it. The purchasing company in London was owned by an old CO of his, ex-rock ape, who did some very discreet brokering for people in his line of work.

He specialized in small team work, infiltrations and terminations, extractions, the odd single job just like the one completed. He tried to keep it close to legal, even picked up the odd snag for the Brit or US government. Nothing in Canada, they didn't know he existed, an out of work Fiber Optics Inspector that worked mainly out of the country and obeyed all the rules. And to help ends meet sometimes brokered for a leather importer in the UK.

The CO could also supply teams of up to one hundred men all trained for assaults, or to train other teams and so forth, quite a lucrative business.

He sent him an email from a café in the airport with a one word code for his success included in the promise of more leather for the future from other companies, as leather was the in thing in today's market and it gave him a good reason to be in that location at that time. All he needed. He couldn't wait to be on his way.

Not to worry, there it was, his flight to Vancouver right on time, he'd be asleep before takeoff. And good Old Blighty with all its pissing rain, behind him. He guessed all that heat softens you up, maybe it was just him, but there were millions of people in London thought it was the capital of the world. He wasn't a big city fan anyway. He travelled tourist and put up with the crying kids, if he scowled enough they usually left him alone, just another overseas worker on his two-in and two-out.

He'd hit Van at 6am Pacific. Picked up the wheels, his pride and joy, a four-year-old Range Rover. It never let him down, well not yet anyway. He had about a ten-hour drive, then an hour hike to his sanctuary, and he couldn't wait to be back there. He needed to be there. He needed time to come down. He'd just done two jobs back-to-back, both loners. It brought the stress factor up and now it was time to bring it down with a little r and r.

His sanctuary, as he called it, was a 3,000-square foot timber frame structure which he had specially built by a well-known prefab builder who specialized in back country ski cabins and snowmobile stop-overs. They would build these structures and fly them in under choppers and that is what they did; two trips, one for the main building and another trip for a small shop or shed, in which he kept a generator and a 500-pound propane tank with lift hooks.

He changed it out once a year, back-up batteries with a solar panel roof, which they dropped down on the edge of a cliff overlooking the most beautiful lake in the world.

Well in his eyes any way. He was roughly five miles to the lake and all this was situated in the central north west corner of a 5,000-acre ranch, belonging to Mel and Linda Armstrong, whom he had befriended a number of years ago while on a hunting expedition. Ranchers hate elk, almost as much as mountain lions. The mountain lion will kill a 1000-dollar steer and eat it, an elk can piss on 1000 dollars' worth of hay that cattle won't touch, it's something in the urine. So which is the worse?

But anyway he chose his property for a hunt and Mel welcomed him, saying kill all you want. Of course that's not allowed, but he offered to knock one down for him if he had a tag and he dug in to his vest pocket and produced his tag for that year. He took it and didn't say a word, this boy was in his late seventies, with a little limp so he wasn't hunting much these days, but just kept getting tags in the hope one would stop long enough for him to get a shot off, from the tractor or his old pick-up which was illegal in both cases. But he figured he was allowed to protect his stock, the elk weren't hard to get, the cougars were a different story.

He spent a week on his property that year and was struck with the beauty and the solitude, the high country was fringing on the Selkirk Mountains or close. It was something God made for himself and he just wanted to borrow a piece of it for a while. The day he left, there was no-one around on the ranch so he hung the bull elk with the tag on it and the horns beside it with two lion pelts on the fence line beside his barn.

Later he found this caused quite a stir. The whole week he was up there, he never saw a soul, never heard anything that resembled a human. Wow! He loved it. He had to leave his ATV part-way and hike the last mile to the ridge where his home was today. This was when he decided that he would like to live there. He didn't know if he could handle it, pretty lonely. But he wanted somewhere, where he could relax and get it all back after a high stress job. On paper he was a Fiber Optic

Consultant or Inspector, whichever he could get. Not a lot of work left in that field unless you wanted to go to Afghanistan and repair broken pipe and fiber, the same piece day after day no doubt. If he went there he wanted to be carrying a gun and wearing combat boots. Not doing fiber.

Mel and Linda had come from their weekly shopping day in town, pulled their old pick-up to a stop in the yard and old Dusty their border collie went round behind the barn and was creating a riot, running back and forward between Mel and Linda and the back of the barn.

"I'll go and see what's got into that dog." Mel said dropping an armful of bags, full of groceries on the kitchen table.

"Linda, Linda come here and see this right now. Damn! I don't believe it, I just don't believe it"

"What?"

She was just scurrying round behind the barn and there was Mel having a conniption, dancing around and laughing like an idiot.

"What's got into you?"

"Look, look! Hanging on the fence, that damned cougar. I thought there was only one but two Damn! Damn! Isn't that great, that will save us some stock. And look at that, a whole elk, all cleaned out and ready to cut. And that kid is gone, just like that. I knew there was something about that lad, the way he handled that gun, just smooth like it was old hat to him and that hunting gear he had, all the latest stuff, but well used. Well just goes to show doesn't it?"

"Oh, I thought you said he didn't look like he could cut it, I must have been mistaken! You old fart."

"Well never mind I'll go and hang that elk a little higher and let it hang for a week, maybe longer. Ha, we will eat well this winter old girl."

It was two weeks to the day when he was back on their door step with his hat in hand. He had done a lot of thinking about that place, and made up his mind he wanted to live there, in the high country. He could always go to Mexico for the winter, if he couldn't handle it. He had a buddy that lived there so no big deal, as the snow got to eight to ten feet any winter, but he didn't think about it.

He'd just rapped on the door when it flew open, he almost rapped old Mel on the forehead and they both just gawped at each other. Mel beat him to it.

"Come in lad, we were just talking about you and hoping that you'd come back so we could thank you for that elk and those cat pelts.

"Pretty good shooting I'd say, now you have to tell me all about every shot and don't miss a thing. Oh and you'll be staying for supper if you can fit it in I hope."

That was when Linda got into the picture.

"We've got the first roast from that elk in the oven right now with all the trimmings, so we won't take no for an answer, unless you've got to be someplace else."

"No Ma'am." That was all I got out.

"Mel, take the lad into the parlor and give him a drink, then ask all the nosy questions you want to ask and let me get on with the supper, it'll be ready in an hour."

And that is how it went with Mel and Linda Armstrong. And for the next hour they talked guns, shooting and every critter that walked the woods. Mel had been quite a hunter in his day and still carried a piece on his tractor. Lots of bear and cougar in that country and if you pissed them off it could be nasty, you'd never know, just get between an old sow and her cub, and look out.

Well by the time supper came around he'd had a couple of Buds and a good stiff Crown Royal, Mel was a free pourer, no measures, no ice. "Just the way God made it," he said.

He'd eaten a lot of wild game in his time but the way that lady prepared it was the best he'd ever had. And he let her know it.

"Stick around lad, that's how we eat in this part of the country."

He didn't know who was playing who, but they were closing in on his reason for being there.

They had touched on his parents, both dead from a car crash on the M1, his Dad had just retired from the Marines after 21 years and they were heading to Europe for their first vacation in a long time. He was deployed in the Middle East when he got the news it blew him away, his dad stood 6' 2" and was in great health and great shape, you don't get to be an RSM in the Marines any other way. It pissed him off no end when his son joined the Regiment as there was only one, and that wasn't it. Wrong mob, RAF Regiment! "We used them for picking up after the Marines," he would say. Yes, they had some words about that!

Mel had gone through the second big one in the

Vandoes, a real mean bunch as the story goes. So they were all old army buddies and just letting it happen. ~~When it did happen! The reason he was there, Linda just~~ up and asked:

"Now what brings you back to our door, Jim?"

You could taste the silence, real good. So he let them have it.

"Well with your permission I'd like to live here, buy a little piece of the mountain and put up a home."

"Where?"

"Up there on the cliffs, overlooking the lake."

"You out of your fucking mind? It gets to be 35 below in the winter, up there, as you put it, and no way to get in or out, there is no road, never was, that is a hundred feet of granite without a toe-hold."

"Well there is a split in the rock you can get through."

"Oh! You discovered that did you? Still what on earth made you think you could live up there?"

"Well I like it up there, peaceful, no people, it's my kind of place.

"Well, no question about that, I've been up there and just sat and enjoyed it myself. You won't get closer to God than that. But, there is a problem! We don't mind where you live, we would be glad to have you for a neighbor, but I can't sell it to you, in the province of BC you can't divide up farmland. Now I know you could never farm that anyway, no-one could, unless you wanted to grow skyhooks maybe."

"Well how about leasing me enough to put a cabin on and allowing me to park here while I'm up there? I won't cause you any problem and I'll help with the haying in the fall, if I'm not working. And probably throw in an elk when the season is open."

He was laughing now as he knew he was not getting to do this, when Mel said:

"OK, if you are crazy enough to try that, I'm going to be crazy enough to let you.

"Now just don't make a mess up there and don't cause no fires as the only way they could fight fire up there is from the air and it would never look the same."

He was in shock, this is what he wanted, he didn't give a shit if he owned it or not, all he wanted was to use it. All he could say was:

"Thank you. Now what will you take for the lease Mel?"

"Oh we'll talk about that later. It'll be something you can afford, don't worry now. Let's have a drink to celebrate our new neighbor. Hey lass, make down the spare bed as he is not driving after drinking, the jail in the 'Stoke is not a nice place. And she gave him a sly look.

"And who would know that any better than yours truly?"

He gave him a funny look and he shook his head.

"A long time ago lad, a long, long time ago. And she will not let me forget it."

And that was the beginning of his friendship with the Armstrongs, that was five years ago. His cabin was a bit of a shock to them when they saw it flying past beneath that big Russian chopper, which was designed for moving large military transport, then sold off to this contractor who used it just for that purpose, moving his cabins onto site. Heli-skiers and snowmobilers loved them and so did he.

He lived on the mountain and kept his boat, a 25-foot cabin cruiser about 10 miles north of the Mica Dam on Kinbasket Lake. He picked the boat up cheap just outside Seattle, it was a repo and needed a lot of work, although the engines, two Volvo diesels, were in good shape.

It had been sunk in a storm and the owner didn't want it back, so engines were rebuilt and the rest was left up to him and that was his life, hunting and fishing and running on the mountain trails, stacking hay for Mel and hanging out on his boat.

A year later, there was a bit of a crisis on the ranch, beef prices had dropped below market value, ranchers were giving it away just to survive. Mel said he didn't know if he could hang on. He was more worried about Jim than himself.

"I'm broke" he said.

"The tractor is on its last legs, the pick-up is fifteen-years-old, shit, if I lose the ranch, what happens to your place up there? The bank will take it all. We got no kids to help out, we wanted some, man we tried but not to be. Right now we couldn't give this place away."

He did some fast thinking and it didn't take long, this was where he wanted to be. He had no family so what the hell was he going to do with it. He had a good nest egg so he made Mel an offer he couldn't refuse, and he didn't. The mortgage was small so he cleared it off and he got some cash to tide them over and they did up some paper work to make it right.

He was a silent partner now with a 50-50 share and if

anything happened to Jim they got it all. He had a buddy in Kelowna, Troy, owned a John Deere dealership with money he had got from the same line of work Jim was in. He bought a brand new brute with the whole loadful, cab air, stereo, nothing missing just for cost. Hey, what are friends for? He had a Ford 1-ton pick-up all decked out that he had taken on trade for a combine so that went on the low-bed as well.

This was all cash for Troy and he delivered on a Sunday, so none of his guys knew those two rigs were gone, sold by him right off the lot on a Sunday. Hey, the boss got lucky sometimes as well and delivered the same day. He got a draft from a bank in Cyprus, had a beer and one for the road and he was on his way home. He passed Mel and Linda coming in the driveway.

Mel said.

"Who the hell was that, leaving like his ass was on fire?"

"Just a buddy of mine, dropping off a couple of things for me."

"Holy smoke what's this doing here?"

"That's a brand new Deere, top of the line."

"Shit like that costs a fortune."

"Well, now that we are partners, you don't expect me to ride on that old pile of shit do you?" and I threw my thumb over my shoulder.

"Whoa, whoa! We can't afford that."

"You can't maybe, but I can. This is just my contribution to tighten up the deal OK. Oh and by the way, get rid of that old pick-up or maybe we could use it for hauling fence posts, but don't park it beside your new one, it makes it look shabby; and he tossed him the keys."

Jim was around the corner before Mel could say anything, and when he peeked back they were both just staring at the big crew cab with all the bells and whistles. Linda just opened the door like she was shoplifting and looked inside, and the tears were in her eyes and Mel was no better.

"My God girl, we are sure going to look like a pair of toffs next time in town."

His first winter in the mountains was an eye-opener, his lodge, as he called it, stood four feet off the ground in the front and about five feet from the edge of a two hundred foot drop to the valley below. He could see for miles, then it started to snow and he thought how beautiful it was. He put tracks on his ATV, two weeks later he bought a snowmobile. By the end of six weeks he was on snow shoes, his three steps down to the ground at the back of his lodge became five steps up.

His view at the front was gone, he was looking at a wall of snow. He was in shock, the snow was ten feet high. He'd stop in town for a beer and a meal cooked by someone else, usually at a place called the 112. Great food, the best in the 'Stoke for his buck, then overnight there, have breakfast at the Pioneer. Nothing like it, you didn't get breakfast like that anywhere else unless it was at home. He'd hear the locals talking about how mild the winter was, only minus twenty and not much snow this year, he was in shock.

He started making plans for Mexico. He loved skiing and there was none better than in Revelstoke, he'd ski three times a week, when he wasn't feeding cattle, almost wore out his snowmobile and it just got deeper. That little town got livelier every night, if you could find a room for the night in season, without a reservation it was a poor season, man they came from Montana to snowmobile there, now that's something. If you've seen the snow in Montana you would understand. By mid-January Jim was loading the Range Rover and headed south for the Baja. Mel got a chuckle, and said who's going to feed the stock? He felt bad about that but he said "don't even think about it, get out of here."

And he was gone. Five days later he was fishing and sucking up sun just off the coast of San Filipe, had a Dos Equis between his bare feet and not a care in the world. He rented a small home on the beach at Punta Estrella, just a little further south on a dirt road, and he wasn't going back till the snow was all gone. Next year he'd stay but he'd be ready for it. He gave Mel a call and he and Linda were still laughing at his quick departure, and marveling at how long he stayed up in his snow-nest anyway. That was his first year on the ranch in his mountain retreat or lodge.

Now, he had one other companion on this mountain, a full-blown timber wolf with a bit of German Shepherd in there, possibly. He didn't own him, they just hung out together. He had been hiking, and overnight camping close to Downie Peak another favorite spot, when he heard this awful noise, whining and yelping, so he went to investigate and there was a pint-size wolf pup trying to take down a rather large fawn. He had hold of its back leg and wasn't letting go, there was kicking, shaking, stomping all going on. He was taking a licking in no uncertain terms, but still trying to eat this thing that was twice his size. This pup was starving and this was a last-ditch attempt at survival. The fawn finally kicked him off and took off into the bush.

This left Jim as the next in line for supper, but he beat him to it and produced a strip of jerky from his pack. He swallowed it whole so he fed him some more, bit by bit and got his finger lacerated for his efforts. Then his granola bar, the chewy kind, that was fun to watch, the fluids were just running out of him as he gave him the whole thing at once, his little head was changing shape as that big bar was moving around in his mouth.

He finally got it crossways and he thought his little yellow eyes were going to pop out, it just stretched his jaws to the max, he could see all his milk teeth just gleaming and the drool was running everywhere.

He just knew he was going to shit his brains out after that, as it was one of those high energy bars to kind of keep you going for a while. After that he had nothing left so he headed out on the homeward trip, not too far, but for a little guy like him it was a long haul and he was right on his heels all the way. He'd stop and look at him and he would just sit down and look back, like they were buds now and that was that. Well, they walked on and heard him bringing up his meal, just puked the whole thing up and bits of grass, twigs, he had been eating anything he could keep down. He lay down and tried to eat it back up but Jim wouldn't let him, instead he tried to put him in his pack and lo and behold he let him. The top was open and his head was hanging out and that was how they made it home. When he took the pack off, he was still asleep and just wouldn't wake up, so he set him down on the porch, still in the bag, still sleeping, got an old pillow and a small dish of water with a little milk in it, cranked up a little porridge and set it down beside him, and went inside to get some supper for himself. After an hour he went out to check on him and he was curled up deep in that pillow and all the food and drink gone.

Now that was three years ago, today he stood three foot tall, and a good 150 pounds maybe more, depending on his little hunting trips or how many fish Jim could catch. A two-pound rainbow could disappear off the deck in minutes, everything! Head, tail and the deck licked clean.

He'd leave on little business trips they called them, could be gone for a month at a time. Now Jim had a hopper that held 100 pounds of kibble. It dispensed two pounds a day at a certain time. If that went dry he was on his own but he never saw him hungry again, after the first time. He would ride in the Rover, in the back as he couldn't fit in the front seat or on top of a load of hay bales. That border collie Dusty never showed up when Tinker was around, and he never heard him bark once. Wolves don't and he guessed that's what he was.

The chores were all done, the hay all stacked. Jim was on his third day fishing and loving it, fall was in the air, a fantastic time in that area. He was low on everything, smokes, beer and even food, so he had to go to town, at least within the next few days, and this time it meant he should check the mail. He had a PC at home on the mountain, satellite of course, but he never used this address on it, never. He used one of the coffee shops with a PC, you just paid your buck and got your 15 minutes.

Like anyone else he'd get email from different parts of the world, but if he got mail from a certain leather company with good deals on sales, or looking to put a temporary salesman back to work who knew his stuff, all it took was an urgent sticker across the ad offering a free gift, he'd delete it, then make a call to a certain number on a stray phone, a wipe-off, they were called. You would pick them up at pawnshops or any place selling shit like that for five bucks or more. Get a ten-dollar chip from the Seven Eleven, use them and drop them and you were in business. He'd been clear for a couple of months and enjoying it, but he knew it would end soon enough.

In this line of work you had to keep sharp. Going to the range and running on the mountain was fine but it didn't make you battle-ready, staying sharp was hands-on, kind of like on-the-job training. If you are a craftsman you will know, doesn't matter how often you read the manual, that isn't going to tell how good you're going to be with the tool. Not till you pick up the tools and you are confronted with the crisis, will you know what your reaction time will be. No second chances if you are playing with guns. The other guy might be good as well. You've got to be better. Up till now he'd stayed on top, he kept in shape, tried to eat right, lots of protein; he was six-feet-two and 140lbs.

2,857 miles or 4,596 kilometres from Kinbasket Lake in BC Canada to Boston Massachusetts USA. Same time, a different place. Another world.

CHAPTER 3

"OKAY GIRL LET'S GET GOING, IF YOU WANT TO SEE THAT byline of yours while the ink is still wet. I want to be on the 1.20 in the next fifteen minutes, and in Charles Street within the hour."

"I'll be right with you Mom, just finalizing my packing. I'm taking my laptop as part of my carry on. Give me something to do on the flight. That's a long way. What time we got to be at Logan?"

"You should be there at least one hour before departure. So we gotta leave here by 5:30am. You will get into Heathrow at some ridiculous time in the morning, probably make Oxford by midday, then you can start driving them insane, as you've done to me for the past year."

"Mom, all I want to do is get it done with. Get the best marks I can get, then back here to good old Boston, take over the magazine and make it pay."

"What the hell do you think is paying for this Oxford education, the tooth fairy? And that's not all little girl, what's this about taking over my magazine?"

"I knew that would get your Boston blood all heated up. Wow Mum, you've still got it."

"Ha! Yea I've still got it and intend to keep it. But a good point. By the time you get back I'll be forty-four, might be nice to take the odd long weekend off. Like a Friday and a Monday."

"What you are saying is, I get to work weekends right?"

"If you put it that way."

"OK, not a problem, I'll do it. I'll live there if you'll let me."

"Well girl, that's what it's going to take. I did it and loved every minute of it, now it's your turn. Get your schooling done and slide right in beside your mom, we'll make a good team."

"I know we will Mom! I just can't wait!"

"Let's go."

"Can I drive? I love that Mercedes, it's like driving a truck."

"Girl, you are full of it tonight, taking over my life, criticizing my car, it's only five years old you know. Come on then, you drive."

"Hate the rain though, especially driving in it, makes everything look so black, and the lights so bright."

"Well you wanted to drive."

"Yeah sure, I can handle it, I just don't like it. OK, here we are, wow look at the parking lot, where did all the cars come from?"

"I think the fat club have the basement tonight."

"There is a story for you Mom."

"I think you have to be three hundred pounds plus to get a membership. We are not quite at that stage yet, my dear girl, now lock up and let's get out of this rain."

It was pouring, so they ran across the parking lot, dodging puddles, ran up the steps into the back lobby.

"Hi Ed, how is Margaret?"

"Just fine Mrs. Lawrence, just fine. Well young missy, last day in Boston and off to good old London and Oxford. We are going to miss you around here you know, oh the wife wanted you to have this, just a little something from us."

"Gee thanks Ed, that is so nice of you. Wow this is real pigskin!"

"Just a little something to keep your hands warm, you will feel the damp for a while then you will get used to it."

"Thanks Ed, they are beautiful. You were in London weren't you, before you came to the States, right?"

"That's right, Uxbridge just outside London, nothing but a short subway ride. That's where I finished up my twenty years with the Mob on the Colour Guard, I was their WO. I had a nice little job on the side, real neat pub on the canal called the Swan and Bottle. It was kind of handy, I could keep an eye on the lads. They liked to grab a pint at the Bottle, good bunch of lads, most times, would get a little rowdy once in a while. But they were just letting off steam, that's all. Get them out in the field though and there weren't any finer troops in any man's army. I served in Cyprus, Aden, which is in Yemen, Bahrain then in Kenya. Met the wife in Nairobi having a bit of r and r, she was a WAAF, what they called the ladies of the Air Force, all good times. Now I'm just boring you, so off you go and enjoy the gloves."

"Thanks again Ed, now don't you dare go and retire before I get back."

"Not a chance dear, that's a date we will keep." And the elevator door closed.

"Now Mom, I'll bet that's a story right there. Ed's been around for a handyman. Don't laugh, I tried."

"You're kidding."

"I'm not, and he wouldn't give. Kept it all vague, I just knew he was being polite so I didn't push it, I'm not going to spoil a friendship for that. But don't underestimate him. That jolly smile could fool you. I watched one night when one of our local hard cases tried to get in, what for I'll never know. Ed just told him, not possible lad, not without an appointment, in that nice manner that he has, this guy tried to just push past Ed. Now I was watching it, but didn't see it happen, that's how fast it was, this guy ended up on the floor and you could hear his arm break, it wasn't a nice sound, anyway this dude was in a heap on the floor squealing and went for his pocket with his good arm, ever-smiling Ed just stepped on his throat and said lad you are making a lot of mistakes tonight, now if you pull out what I think you are going to pull out you are going from a broken arm to a broken neck, and he grabbed the hand and pulled a 38 out of it, and said:

"Well look here, a Saturday night special and it's just Tuesday. Now you go on and get your arm fixed and tell the lads you got jumped by someone better than you. You don't have to tell them he was old enough to be your grandfather, I'll never tell," and he just turned his back and walked inside. Oh I could tell Ed's been around. Here we go, our floor."

"Wow Mom its dark in here, I'll get the lights."

Every member of the small staff was present, just waiting for the lights, that was their signal.

"Surprise!" And the whole place went crazy.

"Wow you scared the crap out of me. Mom, did you know about this? Damn right you did, I know when I've been set up. Oh my God, look at the cake, what a beaut."

"That's not all kid, champagne, nothing too good for my little girl, or partner, whatever way you like."

"Oh Mom, do I have to go? Can't I just stay here and learn from you and Toby and Les?"

"No, go girl, you know it and I know it. That is the secret to this business, today you got to have the papers behind you if you want doors to open for you."

"Well you did it."

"Different time and a different place. How I got this far I'll never know. But with a degree behind you, it makes you a serious contender, and that is what they want to see today, someone who is willing to make the commitment by going to school for a couple of years. And believe me, each school has different points. And the one you are about to enter is the best, also the hardest points to get, but it will make life easier for you and this mag if the top dog went to Oxford."

"OK, OK, I know you are right. It just seems so long."

Toby and Les both chimed in:

"You will be back before you know it."

Toby said:

"I've been on assignments that have lasted longer than you are going to school for, so don't give us the sob story, and ma says that is your desk and it stays right there for you."

"And the minute you step off that plane, on return, I'm your boss and that is when you learn all about creative reporting. By the end of the year you will have so many hours in the air you are going to feel like a pilot yourself, so get ready little girl."

"That school is only the start of your training."

"I can't wait," and the chatter began, all the stories of days gone by, till mom gave the time up signal and said it is time to go.

"On the move early tomorrow kiddo, so you'd better try to grab a couple of hours' shut-eye before then.

"Toss me the keys and I'll meet you in the parking lot, and don't be long. Oh, give me a bottle of that bubbly, Ed didn't make it up so I'll drop this in his office."

"OK Mom I'll be right down." Now this took twenty minutes and she was getting impatient.

"God! What kept you? All you had to do was say goodbye, you didn't have to email the Pope."

"Hey, you know how it is, everyone has to say goodbye in their own way? Those are my best friends Mom."

"I know dear."

"Sally cried for God's sake, I told her, her workload wouldn't be so big now that she didn't have to correct all mine. I think Toby and Les were having a contest to see who could hug the hardest, I thought my lungs were going to collapse. Man those guys are the best."

"Yeah and don't I know it, our mag wouldn't be where it is today if it wasn't for them, those guys could get a job anywhere today if they wanted it."

"Yes they could, but I'll keep the team together, and that is what they like, playing on a team, and they like this team." The car swept into the driveway and the overhead garage doors slid open and closed behind them."

"OK kiddo, let's hit the sack it, will be up and at 'em time before you know it."

"OK Mom, see you in the morning. Love you!"

'Wow I'm going to miss that girl. It's too bad her father couldn't have stayed sober long enough to see what a diamond he had fathered. Well that is something that he gave me that I'm thankful for, and that is all' her mom mused.

It's 4am and mom was drinking coffee and smoking.

"Come on girl got to get going, all it takes is one traffic jam and we're in trouble, got it all now?"

"Yep, passport, boarding pass, yeah. Wow Mom this ticket is business class."

"Hey, moving up, good reporters always go business."

Logan is the main artery to overseas travel in Boston and never quiet, a continuous roll of people and a babble of different languages coming and going and this is what they meld into. Luggage is weighed and checked in, just the carry on left, and that would be scanned before boarding, along with everything else.

"Well girl, this is it, I'm going to miss you more than I can say, you are still my little girl you know, so take care. And go get 'em. I'll be looking for your mail and let's see some good marks."

Her eyes were brimming over but she held it back, but there was no point as her daughter was crying profusely, but quiet and they hugged and held tight for a long time and when they broke, mother smiled and turned and walked away into the crowd.

She wanted to ponder and think about things, how sad, how lonely, how lucky she was. But her flight was called and the droves all scrambled for position for seats that are designated, there is one for everyone, no-one has to stand, never seen it yet.

Once the line was formed they then announced oldies, wheelchairs, and kids, that meant families, they hadn't got around to letting kids on by themselves yet. Overhead luggage stored, all the pods slammed shut, seatbelts fastened, no time for pondering thank God, she thought. Twenty minutes in the air breakfast is served.

Approximately sixteen hours later she was in her dormitory sitting on her bed, bone-weary trying to understand what her new limey roommate was trying to say.

CHAPTER 4

"HEY LOU, HAS THAT KID GOT BACK TO YOU YET, SINCE SHE LEFT?"

"Every day Les, just a line or two, but that's enough, she was going to some party last night.

Some rich folks' kid is laying it all on and she has been conned into going with her roomy."

"Hey, those were the days, right?"

"I suppose so Les, I can't remember back that far."

"Oh bull."

"Mrs. Lawrence, call on line two."

"Thanks Sally. Sally, call me Lou in the office, or anywhere, anytime, OK?"

She grabbed the phone.

"Hallo."

"Is this Mrs. Louella Lawrence?"

"Yes. This is she."

"Mrs. Lawrence, this is Inspector Newton of New Scotland Yard. I'm afraid we have some disturbing news for you. Your daughter was the victim of a drug overdose last night, heroine I believe."

"What? Come again! My daughter? There must be some mistake."

"I'm afraid not Mrs. Lawrence, quite a substantial

amount was found in her possession. We do believe she was supplying and trafficking at this party, and had fallen victim to her own vices."

"Listen to me, buster, my girl has never touched that stuff in her life, so let's cut the crap. Where is she, in custody, or what? No I'm afraid not, it's more serious than that Mrs. Lawrence, she passed away early this morning. Everything was done that could be done, but the amount found in her system was far too great. I am sorry, Mrs. Lawrence, are you alone just now? If so, you should call someone, a family member or a friend."

"Dead? Passed away?"

"Yes, I'm afraid so."

"There must be some mistake, must be! I'll be on the next flight Inspector."

"Very well, Mrs. Lawrence, I will meet you at the airport, whatever time you get in at. You shouldn't travel alone at a time like this."

But she had hung up and was punching a number to Logan Airport. Using her business number she got the first flight out, and a cab to pick her up from her home in an hour. She walked from the office, shutting the door behind her and putting on her coat at the same time. Then shouted without looking:

"Les, you are in charge till I get back, could be a while, OK? So handle it."

"What the hell was that all about?"

"Don't know Toby, maybe the kid is acting up. I've never seen Lou leave like that before. I hope it's nothing major. She will likely be back in a day or so, all full of vim and vigor and crawling down our throats for the deadline. But, from now on, till her majesty returns it is, Sir Les. Got that?"

"Fuck you, sir fucking Les."

There was a chorus of laughter and snickers.

"Damn, a guy can't get no respect around here."

"How the hell did you get to be the Head Editor with grammar like that?"

"It's a knack, my man, it's a knack."

It was a seven-hour flight that she didn't notice, she didn't sleep, didn't eat, but sat and tried to figure it out. How could they make such a mistake, how?

It was going to be all right, everything was going to be a big mistake and someone was going to catch some flak and she would have an excuse to see her daughter without losing face, like the lovesick mother she was.

She nearly laughed, but it was very unusual that Scotland Yard made mistakes.

She cleared customs and was pointed towards Inspector Newton by the customs official. It seemed they had been forewarned to single her out. He was very gracious and asked if she would like to go to her hotel first after her long flight.

"No, I want to get this over with Inspector, I can't believe you have my daughter, I'm sure there is some mistake".

And they swept off in an unmarked sedan with a plain clothes driver. Newton sat in the front and made polite conversation about the flight, weather and compared the traffic with Boston.

"Where are we going Inspector?"

"The morgue, Mrs. Lawrence, we will be there very

shortly, then the worst will be over and I will take you to your hotel."

"I haven't booked one yet, never thought about it."

"Don't worry, I will make a reservation on your behalf, till this is all cleared up."

"Thank you, I would appreciate that."

And they pulled in to a half-empty parking lot, and right to a side door of plain grey metal with three steps going down to it, no handle, just a key opener, then push your way in and it self-closed.

"This way Mrs. Lawrence please, watch your step it tends to be a little slippy sometimes, and always cool. Just a minute, I'll screen this off, no-one around just now, but you never know."

There was a coroner's tag on the drawer with a number on it, which she didn't notice. He grabbed the drawer and slid it out. Then he uncovered the face. She breathed a sigh of relief, it was not her little girl.

Then she gasped for air, as she realised it was, it was her daughter, her only child.

"Oh! My God. Oh! My God. How did this happen?"

She sobbed as she collapsed over the tray.

"What have they done?"

She gripped the cold form of her child and tried to squeeze life back in to it. And the lifeless face was smeared with tears and lipstick and what little make up she had. Her legs could no longer support her, the inspector saved her from falling, his arm around her waist as they left the building.

He helped her into the car and got into the back with her. Nodding to the driver he murmured 'the Strand

Palace' and the car moved off into the London traffic. Her sobbing subsided and she sat in a trance. Newton told her he had taken the liberty of booking a room in the Strand and it was just five minutes away.

She didn't notice, not even when they stopped at the door and he guided her out and into the foyer, he was handed a key by a receptionist. He didn't talk, but glanced at the tag number and took her straight into the elevator and pushed the second floor button and escorted her to 211 the last room at the end of the hallway. He fumbled with the card and slid it into its slot, then removed it, opened the door and escorted her to a chair. He picked up the phone and ordered tea, then disappeared into the bathroom and returned with a glass of water and coaxed her to take some.

The driver arrived with her luggage, and the tea followed, she had regained some composure and took a sip of the tea.

"Thank you Inspector, for everything, but I think I would like to be alone now. I will contact you as soon as I get myself together."

He frowned.

"You should have someone with you."

"No, no thank you, not at this time. I will be in contact with you in a day or two."

"I'll await your call Mrs. Lawrence."

He nodded and left. She watched his car join the other traffic and head in the direction of the Yard then fell on the bed and started to weep again. Great sobs left her gasping for air and it didn't stop till sleep overcame her.

She woke in the night and called room service and

asked for a bottle of Bourbon for 211. She was informed they had two brands, so she told him the first one you touch, send it up.

"It will take a moment Ma'am as it is 3am, we will have to unlock the bar."

"Do it."

By 8am it was gone.

The phone rang offering a room service breakfast which she declined and asked for coffee and another bottle of Bourbon. Before they arrived she phoned the Yard and asked for Inspector Newton. She obtained an appointment for the next morning at 9am. He offered to send a car but she refused saying she would take a cab.

It was the evening of her second day in London and she hadn't eaten since before her flight. She ordered supper and had a shower. While she ate she took some sleepers to get through the night.

Coffee and a cab for 8.45 and she was in the famous Scotland Yard. The uniform was crisp and the name tag said Constable Walker. She gave her name and was told Inspector Newton was waiting, and he led the way to a small office with a glass door. It was on the second floor and on a corner with a window on each side. His desk was set so he could see out of both, with just a turn of his swivel chair. He jumped up and offered her a chair.

"Coffee or tea Mrs. Lawrence?"

"Nothing, I'm fine thank you."

He shook his head at the constable who disappeared and closed the door. He raised his hands for her to speak.

"There are just a few things I'd like to clear up."

"Certainly, where would you like to begin?"

"Well, all I know is that my daughter was invited to a party by her roommate, I believe one of the students was laying on a bit of a bash for the new students, she emailed me and told me about it, and the fact that she wasn't really that keen on going, but would go anyway. Now let me put you clear on one thing Inspector, and don't give me that, I've heard it all before look, because you haven't, not from me anyway. My daughter never in her life has done hard drugs. I say that because we talked about it and she couldn't understand how young people could put their lives in jeopardy over it. She had no desire to try it.

"She wrote an article called 'The Downfall of the Human Race Through Drugs.' It took her six months to complete, it made her sick, just seeing people in the rehabs and the terminal cases in hospital. In that time she visited hospital after hospital, parents of dying and deceased children, it literally made her sick. I tried to get her to drop it but to no avail. She watched the results of perfectly healthy people who had succumbed to drugs, then overdosed and died. Her father was a drunk and that killed him. That article was picked up by the top papers in the US and right here in Britain tabloids waited in line for a piece of it.

"And with that she vowed she would never touch the stuff. Have you got that now Inspector? So, now where do you look for the fall guy, Inspector?"

"Mrs. Lawrence, that was never our intent, but there is a discrepancy already. We were led to believe that your daughter threw the party."

"Inspector, she knew no-one in this country until

she arrived here, her roommate was the first one she had spoken to and had contact with and my daughter couldn't care less about any party. Now Inspector I have said my daughter never did drugs, but obviously she was given them or forced to take them. What I would like to know is by whom? This is your department, Inspector. That stuff was planted on her. And my daughter died because of it, in my book that is murder. And I want that murderer, Inspector, I want him found."

"Mrs. Lawrence, we will definitely be continuing our investigation, there is no question about that, and you will be notified of any progress that we make. If what you say is true, there is definitely a likelihood she was used. We have to define why or what is the reason or motive, and we will get to the bottom of it. We were led to believe that your daughter was one of the principal organisers of this little bash. But now with what you have brought to light, I can see there might well be an alternative motive, now what that is, is our job to find out. The reason is there, we just have to find it."

"One small point Inspector, my daughter didn't die of an overdose. She was killed! That is murder. Where I come from, we hang the bastards or send them to the chair. Now whatever you do with those people when you catch them, I don't care, it will never be enough! Ten of their lives aren't worth the one she lost. As long as you understand I will never be happy with any justice your precious crown hands out. But I will have to live with it. Good-day Inspector, I will be in touch!"

And when he looked up, the last thing he saw was the door slamming. Then it slowly opened again.

"Take that tea now Inspector?"

"Yes I will Constable, yes I will."

"The trouble is the damned woman is right, you know. If we catch them our judges will have to let them go, they will have alibis, witnesses, money, they will never pin a murder charge on anyone for this little lot. If you can afford Oxford you can afford the best. That gives the Crown Prosecutor a pretty tough job. Constable I want the team that is on this job in the conference room in 15."

"Yes sir."

CHAPTER 5

"LES, I NEED THE BEST RESEARCH LAD WE HAVE. AND GIVE him the backup he needs, I want a real digger."

"What's up Lou? Give it to me - and no bullshit. OK, you've been gone three days and not a word, so what gives? Take a deep breath and start at the top. Go."

The silence was long and the sigh was rough. He thought she had gone. But she started and didn't stop till all was told. Now the silence at the other end was just as long, if not longer.

"Lou! Oh God! How did you handle all this by yourself?"

"Not very well, I must say."

"My Lord, it just feels like the other day that she left. Are you OK Lou?"

"Well I don't know, I really don't know. Just help me Les, please just help me."

"OK, we will, set up your laptop, get it turned on."

"I haven't got it."

"Get one, go to one of those geek places, let them load it and get on the net, I'll do the research from this end and it will all come through on the mail. Don't shut it off just let it run day and night, got it?

"Oh, Lou, any time you need to talk just call, any time. Any time!"

"Don't turn soft on me Les, but thanks."

She grabbed her purse and left the hotel and grabbed the first cab that showed and headed for Whitechapel. The ride took ten minutes of intense driving, what the London cabbies are noted for.

It was a small shop that dealt in all kinds of electronics and laptops, with a guy that looked more like a hood than a geek. He sat on his stool, reading and waiting, she walked around the store, all quality stuff.

"I need a laptop. In a rush! Like yesterday."

"Why?"

"No reason."

"Right, over here, this is what you want, all the bits and bytes you could ever need, a bit pricey but it will never let you down."

"That good, is it?"

"Ma, Sony will never let you down, it's the tops, you want it or not?"

"If you load it with what I need."

"Plug it in over there. You got it. Flip it open and let it run. How you going to pay for it?"

"You take plastic?"

"Come on Ma, let's be chums and don't treat me like a bloody fool. I haven't seen real cash since Her Majesty was in here last."

She dropped her card on the counter and asked if she can use the phone. "Sure, over there, under the mags." She grabbed it up and punched in the overseas number for the office.

"Bloody 'ell, you phoning New York?"

"No Boston."

"Shouldn't have asked, should I?"

"Les, I've got it, just loading up the programs and my ID so any time you can start loading me up, don't miss a damned thing. You got it?"

"I'm working on the party list the cops wouldn't give, but I'll get it."

"It was at Dalton Square, that much I found out. The cops told me to butt out, just like hear but don't get involved, we will handle it and the old international one, we will keep you posted. OK Les, get someone on it."

"Toby is on it already, he is running makes on all the new students. Don't know just who went to the party, but he will find out, don't sweat that."

"Ok Les, I will be back in the hotel in an hour, you can reach me on my cell, left the damned thing in the room. If Toby comes up with a list, how I don't know, get it to me and start the breakdown, big bucks, no bucks, mums, dads, no mums, no dads, got it?"

"Got it."

"By the time you get back to the hotel you should have it."

"Thanks Les."

"Whoa! Ma don't waste time do you, write for a mag then, eh?"

"I own it."

"Which one then?"

"The one you were reading when I came in."

"Wow! Don't tell me. I love it, can't get it 'ere though, I've got to have it sent in, or imported if you want the correct terminology, bit pricey mind you, but worth it."

"From now on you get it free, but if that PC lets me down you will never see it again."

"You're on, love."

"OK, Barney isn't it?"

"That's me love, the one and only."

"All right then, could you call me a cab, Barney?"

"It's waiting at the door love. They see you coming in they know you're coming out."

"Just what I need, a geek that thinks like a cop."

"I don't think so Ma, before I was making them I was taking them, you know what I mean? Right you do!"

'Only in good old London. He was a petty thief, now he was a businessman,' she said under her breath, and she climbed the two steps to the pavement and thought likely at one time those steps were up instead of down, maybe a hundred years ago, and she got into the humped-back cab you could only find in good Old Blighty and they took off into the traffic. She gave the driver the address and looked out of the window realizing, for the first time that it was a lovely day. For some, she mused, for some.

After two days of fruitless research nothing, reams of background on everyone or anyone that went to that party or even just walked past. Nothing. She decided to go and visit the roommate who might just throw some light on this, even just something to get a start with, anything would help. She phoned for a rental car and had it delivered to the hotel. She took care of the paperwork in the lobby and phoned Lisa and lined up a coffee date for the afternoon. It was a pleasant drive to Oxford, if you took the time to just look. She guessed this was just the wrong time. The parking lot she pulled into was half-full of high end European automobiles, 'I didn't expect anything else' she mused. 'I hope this little Ford is not going to feel out of place with all this class around.' She saw the coffee shop from the parking lot and knew that meant you could see the parking lot from the coffee shop. 'Been in this game too long,' she thought, 'I've developed a suspicious nature.'

She got out of the car just as a light rain started. She bent her head and briskly headed to the shop. Lisa was tall and sexily dressed, more like a Parisian hooker than a college student. She arose with her hand out. "Mrs. Lawrence, my deepest condolences."

"Thank you Lisa, I'm still numb and find it hard to accept, but it's slowly sinking in."

"You know, if I didn't know you were Laura's mum, I'd swear you were her sister."

"Thanks Lisa, you know flattery will get you nowhere," and they both laughed and she knew she was off on the right foot. Lisa went to get the coffee and came back with one white for herself and black for Lou, this wasn't a normal thing but it seemed to keep her focused. Black and as strong as she could get it, which didn't amount to much in the UK.

"Well Lou, what can I do for you, is there something that I can help with?"

"Well Lisa, anything, just anything. The police are doing their best, but they are not sharing it with me and it frustrates me all to hell. First Laura told me that you had invited her to this party, the cops said different. Which is it? I'm confused."

"I apologise for that Lou, it was me that did the inviting and I've squared that with the bobbies already. Did a number on all the kids that went to the party and there were a lot, quite a number I didn't know. By saying Laura invited me I thought it might just keep me out of the picture, but it didn't. I didn't know anything anyway. But I do know Laura never did any drugs, I'd just known Laura for under two weeks, but I knew she wasn't into that, there were no signs and if she had been, I'd have known right away. I did drug counselling for a year, just waiting to get in here, I've seen them all and it is something you can't hide. Oh, they think they can but seeing them every day, they can't fool you. Ask anyone on campus, they all know who does and who doesn't, it is discussed openly."

"Lisa, who threw that party?"

"Oh that was Louis Martinez, everyone knew that he put up the funds for all the food and booze. Now the smack just appeared, no-one could say who, but we all knew, as only the henchmen seemed to have it. The drugs were just there for anyone to use, all kinds of it, all you had to do was just ask any of the henchmen and you got your lines, no problem."

"Who are the henchmen?"

"That's what we call the Martinez crowd, they were just there and gave it away, Louis never touched the stuff that night, as far as I could see anyway, but I keep away from him, I find him a little too much. But wow did he ever have a thing for Laura."

"Really, tell me about that then."

"That was common knowledge, everyone knew that, as he made a big show of it, you see he always got his way anyway, just snapped his fingers and he had them running. So when Laura just blew him off, he freaked out.

"Even sent a limo one time with roses and she told him no way, and he is quite a looker really, not my type but he always had one on his arm, but never Laura. Just tell me who wears silk suits to class, really, it is just a sea of blue jeans, even those that had an extra quid or so would all try to blend in just a little.

"Not our friend Louis, he didn't give a shit what anyone said or thought, made it quite clear he wanted to be his country's leader someday, and that his dad was grooming him for it, and he also let us know they, the family that is, had lots of clout. Hey, fine, go for it, just don't rub our noses in it. So when Laura gave him the cold shoulder we all felt kind of good, like he had been brought down a peg by one of us. Laura had her goals as well and he wasn't part of them."

"Where is he now?"

She paused, thinking. "Yeah, he went back to Panama, a family crisis or something. Right after the first going over by the cops, he disappeared just like that."

"Do the cops know about this?"

"I gather so, as they didn't even ask for him the second time. And no-one can put the finger on him for being the good guy and throwing a party, if someone brought drugs, that was nothing to do with his Lordship, he would never do anything like that, now would he? And his Dad, making big contributions in all the right places. Wow, all the troubles just go away, don't they? He was going home with a degree, no question about that. You can stay till you do. Don't worry as long as you can pay you can stay, simple math."

"What happened with him and Laura?"

"Oh nothing, he finally got the message after making a fool of himself, called her a Yank Bitch, and she paid it no mind, that didn't help any.

"Got to tell you Mrs - oops Lou I mean, I've got a date tonight and I'm running a tad late, sorry I couldn't have been a bit more help."

"You were lots of help Lisa, I just wasn't getting anywhere with the police and I needed some answers, you have cleared a lot up. Lisa, who is the guy in the corner?"

"Where?"

"Right behind you, across the room."

She turned and looked in the direction of the door and caught him looking at them and he turned away and sipped his coffee, while glancing back.

"Oh the creepy one? That is one of the henchmen, he was at the party. Just like the bloody Mafioso."

"Is he a student?"

"I don't think so, I've never seen him on campus."

And when she looked back he was gone. "Well Lou, got to run now, don't be shy, give me a call any time."

She raised her hand in a thank you gesture. Lou sat and thought while sipping the remains of her cold coffee. It was almost dark and the rain had picked up. She thought it was time to get out of there, thank God for the invention of the GPS, she'd never find that hotel in the dark, but now she'd got some gun fodder for her next meeting with Scotland Yard.

She made it to her car on the run, with the rain turning into a good downpour. She started to punch numbers into her phone and waited for that purr, it was answered on the first ring

"New Scotland Yard, which department please?"

"Homicide. Inspector Newton please."

"The Inspector is not available at the moment, but he will return your call as soon as possible, Mrs. Lawrence."

"Thank you, would it be possible for a 9am appointment tomorrow?"

"9am is open Mrs. Lawrence."

"Thank you."

They didn't even ask her name, it just all came up with the number. Got to give them credit, if this was Boston she'd still be listening to the animated options, press one for this or nine for that. But these cops get the job done pretty fast.

A late supper and at eleven-thirty she phoned the office and caught Les.

"Les, get a rundown on a student, one Louis Martinez."

"You are one step behind Lou, been working on him. The kid is clean, on the surface, at this time anyway. But ma and pa are a different story, nothing you can shout about as they will deny it and they can, it's vague but it is there. Are you online just now?"

"Yes."

"You will have it in fifteen."

"OK, I'll wait thanks Les."

"Call me when it comes through and I'll walk you through it, I'll fill in the blanks for you, bye for now Lou."

She hit the minibar and poured a JD and added some ginger ale. She still had the bottle in her hand when the phone rang.

"OK, look at the photo top left on your screen - Gerardo Moncado Martinez

"That is dad, now all you are getting here is the breakdown. Like first lay-out, still digging up more goodies, this guy is good. If I had his luck I'd start gambling, poor family background, kind of came up the hard way, rather fast though. Partners seem to have ill-fated accidents, nobody's fault just the usual, a car off a cliff, simple things like that, something like you would expect from a nice coca paste kind of guy."

"Hey, got proof of that?"

"Aha! Never can prove any anything, these things seem to happen around this guy. Another little venture, the partner got burned up in an office fire, his wife and kids as well. Lots of business ventures with great success, but they don't match the lifestyle. You know, big houses, cars, planes, now what would he need a fleet of small fast planes for? I can only think of one thing, transporting product. Now that is all we have on him just now, but it is flowing.

"Now! Guess who mama is tied to by blood? Noriega, right, one time El Presidente. Lots of political friends and backs them well, packs a lot of muscle, piss this lady off and you would likely disappear. She never leaves the country and travels with an armed escort at all times, you are not going to catch her out of her own yard, the DEA keep a good watch on both of them, there is something still missing but just haven't got it yet. Well Lou, that is all we have, but it just keeps coming.

"Got a buddy in the DEA, going to give him a call, did him a couple of favors when we were in Afghanistan with the Corps. Maybe it's time to renew old acquaintances and talk about the old days, you know Semper Fi and all that."

"You guys have done great, keep up the good work."

"Thanks Lou, see you soon, I hope."

At 9am she was climbing the stairs at the Yard. It was the same officer at reception and he just pointed to the elevator.

"He's waiting, Mrs. Lawrence."

It was like old hat now and the story was the same now as well. Always very polite, always very courteous, but not getting anywhere and the frustration was building.

"Please sit down Mrs. Lawrence, our progress is a little hampered at the moment as co-operation is not forthcoming, but we are following every avenue open to us."

"Inspector, what you are saying is nothing new has taken place?"

"Not quite true Mrs. Lawrence, your daughter has been cleared of trafficking and there is no doubt that the substance was placed in her possession after her fatality, now why? We have to find that out."

"Inspector, what about this student Martinez, have you looked in to his background?"

"Mrs. Lawrence, young Martinez was questioned

and thoroughly investigated and found to be completely in the clear. He sponsored the party, paid for all the entertainment, food and drink, denied having seen any drugs, if there were any, he said. Now we know there were, don't we? But he has no knowledge of any."

"Inspector, I had a chat with Lisa Thornton yesterday and she is of a different opinion than you about this Martinez."

"Well Mrs. Lawrence I think I'll need more evidence than Lisa Thornton's and her followers, remember she has already given false evidence regarding your daughter. As a point of interest she was rather badly beaten last night and her young man was held and made to watch while this went on."

"How badly Inspector?"

"Well she is hospitalized and will be released later today, I believe. No witnesses as the thugs wore balaclavas. She has not filed a complaint as she doesn't know who to complain about. We have put this down as a jealous lover as there seems to have been a few."

There was a pause.

"Where and when did this take place, in Oxford?"

"No, in Aylesbury, outside a rather trendy night club called the Night Bird, a popular spot for the Oxford crowd, if you have the right cashflow, that is."

"Well Inspector the reason I ask is we were being watched while having our coffee, or I do believe so and when I asked who it was I was told it was one of the Martinez followers."

He leaned back in his chair and breathed a sigh of exasperation and tried not to roll his eyes.

"Inspector, a little more research into his background might reveal that he is not the saint the picture paints."

He raised his hand and intervened.

"Money draws flies, all types, all looking for a little hand-out, this is not against the law. You seem rather well informed, although misled."

She ignored the remark and went on.

"Inspector if the shit don't stink the flies just go away, there are lots of young people at that college with money who don't have followers, it's how you spend it that draws the flies, and this lad seems to draw quite a following, which seems to draw us back to the stink again and the type of flies that will do anything for a buck!"

"A lot of people envy young men like Martinez, with their wealth, it's not their fault their funding is more than adequate. Their families wish them to have all the opportunities they can and if money can pay for extra tuition, or any means of helping them through their studies, then who are we to dispute their decisions?

"Mrs. Lawrence, your daughter was very precious to you and fell victim to a tragic accident that we will get to the bottom of."

Now she stopped him in mid-sentence and her voice was raised with frustration.

"We have been through this before Inspector, my daughter was not a victim of an accident. She was murdered, forget this accident you keep talking about.

"Inspector, my daughter is being flown home Friday and I leave then as well. Her funeral will be Monday. I will contact you Tuesday.

STAN A. COWIE

"When do you expect this Martinez back?"

"Well his family were rather vague about that. But he informed us that he will be in contact with us as soon as he returns, that is all I have at the moment. But I do believe you are barking up the wrong tree in that area, Mrs. Lawrence, any drug trafficking in the UK is not treated lightly, and our drug squad work hand in hand with your DEA on all international matters, so please allow us to do our job and any solid results will be immediately passed on to you. Please allow me to offer my deepest condolences to you at this time, there is no greater pain than the loss of a child."

And with a subdued 'thank you' she rose and left.

Once back in her hotel room she kicked off her shoes and lit a cigarette, not a heavy smoker but just couldn't quite kick the habit. She flopped onto the bed and pulled up her cell.

"Hi Les, didn't think I'd catch you. Having any luck?"

There was a slight pause and he cleared his throat.

"This guy Martinez is one piece of work, stinks to high heaven but smells like a rose. I talked to that buddy of mine in the DEA and he was a little tight-lipped about it, but let a few things go for old-time's sake, you know. Seems they have a little group in Panama, just like here, they call them The Untouchables, bad guys in high places, they won't touch pocket change unless it has been through the laundry at least twice, everything is clean.

"Mama is a little different, she won't leave home because she can't. They are watching for her, she is the bad apple, pointed the finger too many times

58

and - poof - people have disappeared. The Cartel is her church and she is in high standing there and believes Panama has everything she wants: the limos, high-living banquets, El Presidente wouldn't dare throw a party without the Martinezes being there, it just wouldn't be the thing. This family hasn't got enough fingers for all the pies they are in. It all leads back to drugs and that is as far as we have got. My buddy started to dry up after that, wouldn't give much more, said it wasn't worth his job.

"Although he did say the DEA had run a couple of undercover ops in Panama, all small stuff, they felt it was all set-up for them, they had lots of fall guys around. When they did their raids it was with the blessing of the Panamanian enforcement. Martinez was one of the first to congratulate them and the take was all small stuff, they felt it was put on for them. A waste of time and good US tax dollars so no more till something good is on the block."

"Well Les, you have done great. What about any other students?"

"Nothing, we scanned them real good, no busts for anything, the odd speeding ticket, nothing, only Martinez keeps coming up with more."

"OK Les, see you Friday, I'm beat, got to get back home. Can't function away from the nest any more. Must be getting old or soft, whichever."

She had a restless night so rose early, showered, and while drying her hair called the hospital in Aylesbury and found Lisa was released the evening before. She then tried her home phone, got no answer and left a message to get back to her as soon as possible, and also left her cell and home number.

Breakfast, then checked on the arrangements for the transport, flight and all the paperwork, mostly taken care of by Scotland Yard. All in order, be in Boston for Saturday, late morning. The office had been notified that it was closed Monday for the funeral, checked with the crematorium, the Heavenly Night, notified them of the arrival time for the pick-up and transportation of her daughter and preparations for Monday. This was all numbing to her and reinforced the sadness that had never left her. Made a quick call to Barney and told him his mag is all paid up for the next twenty years, and listened to him whoopee with joy.

"Listen love, any time old Barn can help, just ring the bell and make the call, I'm not shy of a little snooping for you."

She thought that one out.

"Barney, I will definitely take you up on that, I'll let you know and the ride won't be free. Thanks Barney."

It was a real scramble, early lunch, then the airport, trying to make it an hour before departure, they like two, but out of the question. The flight gave too much time to think and it hurt. Breakfast was over and the landing instructions were given. It could be London, cool and raining, it didn't help the mood. She decided to go to the office just for a quick look in. A cab took her straight there and dropped her at the door. She was surprised to see Ed up on a ladder, changing a fluorescent light bulb."

"Don't you ever take a day off Ed?"

There was surprise in his voice.

"Mrs. Lawrence! I just didn't know when you would return."

There was a little pause and he said:

"Before you run up, could I have a little word with you?"

"Sure, Ed not a problem."

He came off the ladder and walked close to her and guided her away from the entrance.

"What is it Ed? Something wrong?"

"Well, I know what you have been battling with, this terrible injustice. It is the most horrible thing a parent could go through, as my wife and I both know, we lost our son ten years ago.

"He was in the Marines and we were so proud of him, he was killed by a couple of yobs while on leave in London, so we know the grief you are suffering."

She was quite taken aback as she didn't know Ed even had a son.

"Ed I didn't know, you never talked about it."

"No, well what I really want to say is there is so little the police can do with their hands tied by all that bureaucracy and red tape, and even if they catch the culprit, the punishment will never fit the crime, never! That we know and if this criminal is from out of the country, it's over, oh the books stay open but that doesn't help, not a damned bit! But there are people who can see that those responsible do get punished. It is a little underhanded sometimes but results are usually prompt, and severe, I might add. Now I'm not suggesting you go this route but I'm just letting you know it is available.

"And if you get to that stage and are dissatisfied with

the results up to that point, I could make a call for you, and that is all I have to say, Mrs. Lawrence."

She was a little shocked and didn't know what to say.

"Thank you Ed, thank you so much, I will definitely keep that in mind. What exactly happened to your son?"

"Well, it's just like I said, he had been on leave in London, I had given him some of the hot spots I used to frequent, he had been to the Swan and Bottle out in Uxbridge and had a right old time. Seems he just walked through the door and old John the 'keeper shouted to his missus,

"Rose, I'll bet that's Ed's lad, and they gave him a right good time. They were awfully kind folks, he phoned me right from there in the middle of the night and said Dad you must have been a right old radge, with all the stories I'm hearing, it seems everyone here knows Sargeant Ed, you old bugger, and we laughed good and hearty at that. He was dead one hour later."

Ed's eyes were glassy with the tears from memories of the past.

"And the only satisfaction I got was that some other lads passing by saw what went on and beat the shit out of those two before the bobbies arrived and arrested them, then charged the two young soldiers with assault. They didn't even know our Bobby, but if you were in the mob or the service you looked after each other. I thank those lads every night for the licking they laid on those damned thugs and I think of our Bobby every day. Those two got sent to drug rehab because they didn't know what they were doing, they were out in less than five. Not much punishment there, is there? Now some might think that is just, but I live with the hate inside me, day after day.

"I don't think you want that, do you Mrs. Lawrence?"

There was a pause.

"My God Ed, I didn't know, I never knew, I'm so sorry, so sorry. Tell me Ed, why didn't you make that call, if anyone had a just reason it was you."

"Oh Mrs. Lawrence, that was in the UK and I didn't have the money, it takes a little more than I had. A lot of those lads won't work in country too dangerous, they would likely end up in trouble and they try to avoid that. Now you go on up and get back to work, it helps just a little. But you keep in mind what I said."

"Thanks Ed, but I'm sure Scotland Yard will take care of things. Oh I'm sure they will they always do their best. I'll give the Bobbies that."

CHAPTER 6

A SUBDUED HUSH FELL AS SHE ENTERED. SHE DIDN'T LOOK either way and walked to her office, feeling a stranger in her own domain. Slowly the chatter returned, but the lightness was gone. Half a dozen staff members scooted around trying to get loose ends tied up before going home. Saturday was always a light day but always a skeleton crew just in case something came up. There were three field reporters on overseas assignments but unless it was crucial they knew to leave Saturdays alone, by noon there would be two on call, the rest will have gone home.

She hit her 'com.

"Les, Toby, could I see you before you take off?"

Saturday usually meant they were not there, but today was an exception.

"Sure thing Lou, I'll get Toby and we will be right in."

He moved around his desk and headed for the balcony. This was a portion of the building that only went up the three storeys, the rest went to twelve so it was facing the alley, the building across the way had no windows on this side so it was private. They had an old patio table with a plywood top, kind of blistered from heat and rain and the last remnants of paint peeling off it, an ashtray full of yesterday's butts and rain, half a dozen plastic white lawn chairs scattered around an old couch under the overhang. Toby was hanging over the rail looking down onto the parking lot making big clouds of smoke in the damp air."

"Hey Toby, Lou is back."

"Yeah, I saw the car in the parking lot. How is she?"

"Can't tell, looks a little gaunt though."

"Well I'm not surprized, I didn't expect to see her in today."

Les shook his head.

"I did and she wants to see us before we take off so let's get it done and be gone" and Toby flipped his butt out into the air and watched it spin to the ground."

"Well let's go see, maybe she wants to throw in the towel."

Les rolled his eyes.

"Now you don't really believe that do you?"

"No, not for a minute."

And they both headed for the door. Les tapped on the frosted glass and poked his head in.

"OK now, Lou?"

She waved them in, with Toby bringing up the rear. That was a difference they had, Les called her Lou, Toby called her Boss, always.

"Grab a chair."

They both slumped on some good hard office furniture, Toby said:

"How was the trip Boss?"

"Didn't notice really! But I got to say I'm impressed

on that Martinez file. That is one busy boy about town, and you say the DEA can't pin anything on him? That amazes me, it seems so obvious."

"Well that is not enough, you can't go stomping around someone else's country with just, I think it's obvious."

"I know, I know!"

"This family backs the government heavily. El Presidente lives well beyond his means. The Untouchables again, it gives them a free-hand almost. Just can't get behind that wall."

"What about the kids?"

"There are two, a girl and the boy. Now the little lady is a bitch, you couldn't buy her into a school in the Bronx with a truck load of bucks. They got her tucked away in a low-ender in Amsterdam, she does it all, caught her screwing a teacher and doing coke, smokes weed on a daily basis, but who gives a shit, it is Amsterdam right, been suspended three times.

"Threatened with expulsion, but Dad keeps showing up with another bucket of money. I think he has just about rebuilt that school on his own. Oh yeah, that teacher, she was fooling around with was married, they found him floating in the canal. Suicide! No big deal, right?

"Now numero uno son, this is our boy, you have never seen anything so clean, high grades. Very popular, in all the right places, this kid is going far. Takes Political Science Business Admin and every course that points to politics. This is the family golden boy. Will cost dad a few bucks here and there to keep the shine on, that is.

"Beat the shit out of a kid in UCLA, messing with his lady. Dad paid all the other kid's hospital bills and paid for him to go to another college closer to his home, one he couldn't afford, compliments of the Martinezes. Never made the papers, not even the college rag. Nobody is going to pin anything on that lad, no way. Sorry Lou but that is how it looks."

"OK Les, anything else?"

"Well, Mama is one bad lady, she points the finger and you are going down, totally ruthless. Her family goes back with the Cartel, related to Noriega down the line somewhere and proud of it. What happened to him was a total injustice. Get the picture? If you spilled a drink on her shoes at one of the shabby parties they go to, she would likely have you blown away, then send flowers to the funeral along with the cleaning bill."

"Damn, all that work and nothing to get the hook into. That's it guys, great job, Have a good weekend. Oh Les, could I just have a moment more of your time?"

They both rose to leave, Les said:

"Sure. I'll catch up with you Toby."

"Don't worry, got a few things to clear up. Bye Boss" and he closed the door.

Les sat back down and asked:

"What's up, Lou?"

She had a worried look on her face and shook her head a little.

"I don't know Les, you know Ed fairly well, right?"

He screwed up his face a little.

"Well we had him and his missus over for dinner a couple of times and yeah, he is a great guy, lots of fun, knows all the jokes, but you only get what he wants to give and his old lady is the same way, only once he let slip that after he was out of the forces he let slide that he was involved with M15 for a couple of years, kind of cleaning up loose ends for them, whatever that meant and he didn't go any further. Why"?

"Well he told me about his son, and it was a hard thing for him to do, I could see that."

He shrugged.

"Well he gave me that story, then went on about not getting any satisfaction from the police because their hands were tied and all, but I could get it from another source, from like out of the country, you know what I mean. He was referring to men that had no borders. Then he said he could make a call on my behalf to an old friend that took care of things like that. They would find out, regardless what country."

Les's eyes were wide open and he was sitting up straight. He said:

"What? No no, don't repeat it, I heard you. Holy shit, I just knew that old bastard had a background, I just knew it! Well regardless Lou, you don't go there, no way! OK, you do know what he is talking about don't you Lou? I mean, you know he was talking about mercenaries, Soldiers of Fortune, they are fucking outlaws! Ruthless, deadly, fucking cowboys. Yeah they take care of business all right. Little matters the CIA, DEA, FBI wouldn't go near or can't because of rules. You see they don't have any. Yeah any country you like, Iraq, Russia, don't make no difference. Wow cagey old bastard. Now girl, I'll tell you, just forget you ever had that conversation with Ed. OK?"

"Come on Les, that stuff doesn't still go on, does it?"
He gave her a bewildered look.

"I can't believe I'm telling the owner of a worldly magazine this. It has never stopped from the beginning of time and it will go on till the end of time."

"Les, I thought that was GI Joe stuff and not real, things they wrote comic books about."

"Let me tell you a little story that happened in late 2011, yeah, about three years ago if I'm right. You remember that guy, let me think, yeah Espinosa, remember he ripped off that A.R.T. corporation for millions? They were manufacturing weapons for the US armed forces, high tech stuff, right over our heads, well he ripped them off for millions and killed the president on the way out of the country, I guess he found him out and was turning him in, but bought a bullet in the back of the head instead."

"I sure do, it was the headlines for a while."

"Well he escaped to Columbia, set himself up in Bogota. Then got involved with the Cartel, why else? Bogota. Then he got killed in a fire in his home, the whole family."

"That's right, I remember they perished in the blaze as well, that's the guy."

"What they didn't tell you was that they were all shot between the eyes. They claimed he pissed off the Cartel. Not so, he was their bright star, lots of connections in low places. No no, not the Cartel. It was traced back to A.R.T. Corporation by the CIA. They didn't know for sure and no solid proof, but a bunch of money changed hands and disappeared. And the new President of A.R.T. Well, guess who? The Number One Son. Oh my! He just happened to be an ex-Navy Seal, now those boys knew all the contacts. You killed my dad, think you are getting away with that? Welcome to the dark side and he makes a call while sitting in his executive office, and business is taken care of."

She shook her head.

"Don't the CIA get pissed off at that?"

"They sure do, they don't like citizens taking the law into their own hands, but prove it - they couldn't. And it closed the file on a dirty little scandal. Justice was done."

"Well well, that blows me away. I thought I knew a little! But I know nothing about that life, you live and learn."

"Damn Ed."

"Yeah, I think I'll let Scotland Yard take care of it, I just wish they would get on with it.

"Toby is going to be thinking you have forgotten him. Have a good week end Les."

And the door closed behind him.

Monday was the funeral, with a light reception at the funeral home. It was a cremation, something she believed in, it drizzled rain the whole day, at least no-one had to stand around a grave. Wednesday she was going to work but didn't. Scotland Yard sent an email "doing everything possible, expecting a break soon." Same as nothing. She placed a call to Lisa to see if she had mended after her beating.

It rang three times before she answered and it was a little hesitant, "Hi Lou."

"Hey Lisa, I'm just calling to see if all is mended after that little accident you had."

"No accident Lou, not at all, that licking was because I talked to you about Laura. That yob and his mate told me to forget you if I knew what was good for me. And if it happened again it could be a lot worse, maybe fatal. That is why I'm a little reluctant to talk to you. But it can't harm nothing if no-one knows, right, and you are back in the US aren't you?"

"Yes I am."

"Well I'm not worried then."

"Tell me, did that Martinez get back yet?"

"Oh yes, struts around like he owns the place, just like nothing has ever happened, throwing another wingding this weekend, supposed to be better than ever. And him just got back the other day, never mentioned Laura, not a word, like she didn't exist, bloody greaser, can't stand him. But I'm going to the wingding, why not, His Bloody Majesty."

"OK Lisa, I'd better let you go and get on with things, we'd better say nothing about this call to anyone."

"Not a word Lou, nout, zilch."

"Hey, give me a call sometime and if you need a job I'll fix you up."

"Right on Lou, thanks. Bye."

The phone never touched the cradle and another number was punched in. It barely rang when it was snatched up and a cockney voice came back at her.

"Barney's Computers, what can I do you for today?"

"Barney, I don't know how you can stay in business talking to your customers like that."

A slight pause then:

"Hey, my Lady from Boston, you are not going to

cancel my mag are you? That little trinket the Sony still doing its job then?"

"No problem Barney, it purrs like a kitten."

"If it is doing that send it back, I'll fix it. Just joking Mrs. L. Listen, Mrs. Lawrence I didn't hear about your loss till after you'd gone and I'm awfully sorry, it must have been a terrible blow."

"Yes it was, Barney and it will never go away, I will have to live with it for ever."

There is an uncomfortable moment then Barney comes to the rescue.

"Well Mrs. L, what can I do for you?"

"Well I've always thought of you, Barney as a bit of a party animal, now would that be right?"

"That I am love, that I am, like a pint on the weekend, maybe a little bit of weed and a bit of fluff to keep old Barn happy, now that is not too much to ask is it? You're trying to get a date with old Barn are you? Sorry love, got to tell you, I'm all booked up."

There was a bit of a chuckle on the other end.

"Sorry to hear that Barney, we'll make it another time.

"OK Barn, tell me how would you like to go to a bit of a bash out in Oxford? I'll pay for some yuppie clothes to get you all decked out so you blend in all right. All you have to do is look around and let me know what is going on and enjoy, sound fair and getting paid to boot?"

"Well what's up then love, want old Barn to do a little snooping then? This is not a problem, I get invited out there all the time, that crowd like to keep their high tech gear up-to-date and the cash is no problem, so I keep them happy. Just let's have the rundown so I can get clued in, OK love?"

So she told him the whole story, end-to-end and it brought it all back in a rush. She felt light-headed and had to hold on to the chair, but got it finished, then reminded him."

"This is not a game, be careful, I have big suspicions about this crowd, especially this Martinez, take no chances and don't call me from your own phone, use an outside line, anything, but not yours. Funny thing, there is a bank of payphones inside Scotland Yard that should do it I'd think, just round the corner from your place."

"Trying to scare old Barn love, can't be done, been to the dark side and came back no problem. Listen love, you have been up front with me so I'll give you the same courtesy.

"I've got a lap here that just happens to have no numbers, no address and I can use a different local every time, so it will never come from me. Now I'm going to send you a little code, really simple, I'll fax it to any number you give me, it will be seven pages, one page for each day and a lot of numbers that won't mean much. This was a code they used in the Second World War, my old dad flew the Spitfires in it and never let me forget. But he gave me this code, so simple it will make you laugh, but you can't break it. Bullet-proof, learn it and toss it. So get me a number and I'll send it. The only down side is you won't be able to hear my sexy voice from now on, but I'm sure you can live with it, all right then."

"Got it Barney, I'll let you go. By the way, did you ever work for MI5?"

"Don't they wish, love. Bye."

And he hung up. Wow, friends in low places! There had been nothing from the yard so she let it ride, just no point. A fax number was sent to Barney, from a laptop in Staples the following morning and she received her code by the evening. Seven pages with a note on the bottom of number seven, 'it won't stop a pro hacker but it will slow them down and use up some of his time and really piss him off to boot. Good luck, the Barn.'

She waltzed in and headed straight for her office, a good morning guys and kept on going.

"Wow looks like the old Boss is back Les, I'm glad to see."

"I'm not Tobe, something's going on I tell you, she is up to something, guaranteed."

"I guess it's that suspicious mind that made you such a reporter, right?"

"Hey back to work ma man, someone here has to see that the bills get paid."

"Listen to this, guy, you are making more than you ever made, me too, we got it good, no question, good check and never leave home."

The week moved on by and nothing changed, Sunday morning 6am, baggy sweatshirt and pants, flip-flops and her first cup of the day. She hit the fire-up button on her PC and waited for the password call, typed it in and waited for her mail, she sipped, and scanned it as it rolled by. 'An easy way to improve you sex life.' What's that? Delete! She shuffled in to the kitchen to top up her caffeine intake and light a Marlboro, then strolled back to check the rest half a dozen office memos, ticked them off for delete and hit the button. Next an ad from Alcatel offering all their latest prices for overseas service, new fibre optics submarine cable from Spain to the west coast of Africa. What is this all about? Then she reached for the delete, then froze. Something not right and why, and she fumbled through a pile of papers and came up with the coded sheets, Sunday right and she shuffled the seven pages till the right one was at hand and started counting lines and ticking off words. It took fifteen minutes with a printout to get it all and she sat back to read the message. Her coffee was cold and the smoke was a long line of white in the ashtray.

'Good bash, substance available, large variety, the in-crowd only. No question Mr. P involved in supply, two toughs on hand, not students, kept people from interfering with Mr. P. Oxford Gazette page two.'

They had decided to call Martinez Mr P, short for Panama, just to keep the message short.

What did this mean, Oxford Gazette? She brought up her paper file, she had almost every paper in the world and typed in Oxford Gazette, then page two, and started to read.

'Hit and run takes the life of Oxford Student Lisa Thornton. The victim died en-route to Oxford General, she never regained conciousness and was dead on arrival. Her parents and close friends have been notified and wish for the guilty parties to come forward and accept responsibility for this tragic accident. The police believe juveniles were responsible and alcohol was a factor. The vehicle was found abandoned, stolen from a home in Belmont Place.

The owners are presently on vacation in the Channel Islands and have been notified.'

She couldn't read any further as her visibility was completely blurred, the tears were flowing out of control. She wiped her eyes and tried to read it again, but failed, knowing it wouldn't change.

I killed her, I know I killed her, oh my God, what have I done? I have taken the life of a completely innocent person. She must have had her line tapped or something. Must have! They didn't like her talking to me, so now they have stopped it. She ran from her office to her bedroom and fell on the bed sobbing.

After an hour she emerged wearing blue jeans, a sweater and Nikes and headed for a side door into the garage where the Mercedes sat, with a Lincoln Navigator and a Corvette, toys she had bought in weaker moments. The 'vette she had planned to give to Laura but held it back scared she was spoiling her. She slid into the Mercedes and hit the start and waited while the door rose. A pair of dark shades hid the puffiness around her eyes, getting to be a habit, she thought and turned and headed down the cobbled driveway and through the electronic gates, hung a right and headed for the interstate.

It's a ten minute trip through a nice rural development, she had got in on the ground floor and cornered a secluded lot, they were all one, two and three acres, hers was two and on a small rise, just a little higher than most and well-treed with pine, oak and filled in with sumac. This was her sanctuary, it had been a struggle for a long time, but now all clear, after fifteen years and she loved just coming home to it, at the end of the development, you hung a left and you could see the on-ramp. There was no street parking allowed so there were no street cars behind her and as she sped up the on-ramp, she glanced again in the rear-view, nothing.

She was definitely getting paranoid and she pulled over two lanes into the commuter lane and held it at eighty-five. It took fifteen minutes and she exited the freeway and five more and she turned in to a gravel drive, almost obscure with elm and oak, and trundled down through the potholes and puddles. It opened out into large lawns and white fences. A large stately Tudor home filled a good portion of the clearing, with stables, guest houses and other outbuildings, she parked in the middle of the open lot and started to head in the direction of the home when she was greeted by a loud voice calling her name.

"Hey! Lou, what's up?"

A young man dressed in jeans, baggy polo-necked sweater and rubber boots, carrying a half-bucket of oats.

"Joseph, I didn't recognise you, you are really looking the part, what gives? The hired help quit on you?"

"Gave them the day off just so I could keep my hand in and I love it, all this mucking about, but you didn't come all the way out here to see horses now did you? So let's walk and you can fill me in, see if I can get some money out of you.

"Let me see, we scanned your offices no more than a month ago, right? So what can it be?"

"Well Joseph, I do more and more work at home now and I've had a little scare, so I want the whole place from the curb to the back all secure, full meal deal, cars as well, nothing left out. I want my phone lines set up so I can scramble a conversation if I wish, the bug hunt, from the closet, to the front door."

"I've got a feeling there is a little more here than you are saying, but that's all right, not my affair, right? Just my job to make it right. And secure! And that we can do."

"That's great Joseph, I couldn't ask for more, it's been quite a concern lately with two companies working on the same story, it can get a little dirty, I guess it's the name of the game. I'd hate to see stories my guys have travelled halfway around the world to get showing up as someone else's print first, especially when it costs me thousands. If they want to copy or tear it apart after, go for it."

"OK that's it, is it? As long as I know exactly what you want I can do a thorough job for you, I can set you up with a system no-one can touch, the CIA would have a problem, even then you would know they were coming, or been there. You can check your own phones every day yourself, I'll set it up so it is simple and quick, then once a month we do it A to Z, you will have to do your dry cleaning real simple with a little hand scanner that we supply."

"Do you think that will be necessary?"

He just smiled.

"Absolutely, dry cleaners are one of the best inlets a good snoop can find."

"OK that's it, do it all, I'll feel a lot better. I know they are all doing it, it's old hat isn't it?"

"Lou, none of those people want anything stolen.

One of the biggest soft drink guys in the business is our client and there isn't a gadget out there he doesn't have. Just think, you are opening a brand new factory in India, you do all the leg work and find your competition just beat you to it, that could cost you ten or twelve million, just because he got it from you. Dirty pool, you bet. Our accounts go all over the world now. We are known as one of the top ten and we work at it. All my field ops have past experience, CIA, DEA, FBI, you see I steal as well!"

"Well I always knew you were a rogue, Joseph, just tell me how you steal from the CIA or the FBI for that matter?"

He rubbed his forefinger and thumb together.

"Same way every time, they hate me there, the old greenback still works, I see a good man, I pay him what he is worth and I get him. I have to fight."

"I can believe it."

"Hey! Just a minute, how did you get Les and Toby? Don't tell me, I already know, both their last employers are my clients and I might say they really miss them, but they are really pissed at you so watch out, they might try to hire them back."

A big smile from her.

"They already have, with no luck I'm glad to say."

And he smiled.

"Play the game or pay the price, the new kid on the block better be tough or I'm going to eat him up, right."

And they walked on in silence.

"Wow, remember it like yesterday when we both went into business, same year. I knew you would make it but never this big," and she shook her head.

"Well Lou, I had my doubts about you till you got rid of that husband of yours, then it was all go, I could see the determination and the willpower, there was nothing going to stop you."

She nodded and laughed and he joined in.

"Yeah, two new kids on the block and we both made it. I love this country, nowhere else in the world could you do this, I count my blessings every day."

"Well Joseph, thanks a million for looking after me."

"Be at home Monday for the whole day, I will have a crew there at 8am sharp. Make a note of all your little fears and hidey spots, they won't laugh at them, but they have to know, how big is your place, an acre?"

"Nearly two."

"Good, there will be a crew of six or eight, they will go over every little step of the way with you, then next week I will drop down and fill in all the blanks and show you how things work. Not too much, I don't want you as my competition, I wouldn't be able to handle it."

She thanked him again and hugged him, got to her car, waved and left.

She phoned Les at home and told him the story, why she wouldn't be there Monday and she decided to take a real interest in this project. She emailed off a coded message to Barney, with a thank you and placed a thousand dollar cheque payable to a bank in London, inside a magazine and dropped it in the company outgoing mail, this took place Tuesday afternoon, after the crew had left her place.

They still had two days' work to do they said, cameras in trees and mounted inside fence posts, the house had all been wired with fiber optics, state of the art, then wired in to the police station and also to the alarm company, and the sign said armed response. Impressive, that alone would scare me away she thought. She could sit and watch the TV and at the same time could scan every nook of her yard, front door, back door and every room in the house from the same chair and remote.

At the office she had made up her mind on her next move and as she left she was looking for Ed and caught him just heading out of the door. After Ed left the building you had to use a key pad to enter and sometimes it wasn't the best. Anyway she shouted to him and he spun around.

"Oh hello Mrs. Lawrence, I almost missed you."

"Well I missed you this afternoon, so we are even."

He waited for her to catch up.

"Now, what can I do for you?"

She looked into his eyes and said:

"I've given it a lot of thought Ed, and I want you to make that call."

He just nodded - and he thought now maybe we will get rid of that pain just a little. She headed for the Navigator, her first lesson, rotate your vehicles, why not? Use them, get used to them. Ed headed for the gate and thought 'I wondered just how long it would take.' There's an internet cafe beside the bus stop and he popped in and got a coffee and fifteen minutes. He placed on a pair of reading glasses and dug in his wallet for a business card of a London firm that advertised special leatherware and he placed an order.

He then rushed out as his bus pulled up, 'can't be late

tonight, it's another birthday' the last one just felt like yesterday. How time flies, there never was a call to make.

Two days later there was an ad on the internet to preferred clients. It offered a fantastic deal in the latest Savile Row styles in leather. One of those ads had an emblazoned flash across it, 'Urgent act now and receive a free gift.'

These ads were sent to thousands of preferred customers each month, but to certain customers they meant something else.

CHAPTER 7

"TOMORROW KID, WE GOT TO GO TO TOWN, I JUST CAN'T live on fish and I like my eggs and bacon. So a.m we are out of here."

First light, with a back anchor, he was moored fore and aft, and climbs in to the Rover with that great big head hanging out of the window.

This thing loved to go to town and intimidate all the little rotties and dobies, he never barked. Wolves don't, he just stood and stared and they have a conniption, hair all standing up, pissing all over. He would rush the fence and watch them falling over each other to get away, like he was going to come right through the chain link, but most times he just slept, looked good and knew it.

It was a two-hour trip, more or less, to Revelstoke, first stop the Frontier to take care of business, the best breakfast in town, then the internet coffee shop, the only one in town - two PCs, both so old they could have been made out of wood. They both sit on a large folding table, each one inside an over-sized cardboard box with the tops cut off, so the other guy can't see what you are doing. Pretty smooth really, considering they are back-to-back. The coffee is the shits, but there is always some loafer sitting drinking it. Not much light, just fine with him and two of those old big monitors with the green screen. How he still remembered to work it, he didn't know, with his PC he could get running in seconds, this dinosaur took the fifteen minutes to just heat up and that was OK, gave him time to look around, the owner, the coffee drinker and him. He knew he sold weed on the side to subsidise his income, good job or he'd starve. He pulled up his mail on this address he rarely used, and lo and behold this leather ad. Shit, he just didn't want it right now, but duty called, well the check usually had something to do with it as well.

Now this saved him doing groceries, going on a trip to good old London, fuck, hunting season was just around the corner as well, sure as hell he'd miss it. And he deleted the message, closed up and rose to leave and the old guy said:

"Short and sweet, eh?"

"You got it."

And he was outside and heading for the truck, going to pack and be on his way to Kelowna and catch an evening flight to Vancouver and a Red Eye to London. He didn't get jet lag, he slept like a baby on-flight, it was a fast trip home, he overfed the dog, filled the hopper, phoned Mel to fill him in and he was gone.

It was a five-hour ride if you rushed it from the ranch to the airport and he was making reservations to Vancouver and London as he drove. You've got to watch the cops in Canada, they'll write you a ticket for driving with a cell stuck to your ear, then all you have to do is tell them you are in a hurry, and they will diddle away an hour asking stupid questions and just generally fuck you around. Maybe it was just him, he never met a cop he liked yet, so what was the point?

He made Kelowna, stuck the rig in long-term and ran to the terminal, screamed through the electronic scanners, bells and whistles going off like he was delivering homemade bombs, when you are in a hurry it all goes wrong. Big belt buckles, wallet in back pocket, a handful of change he forgot to drop in the plastic bucket, then the little security guard asked him if he'd ever done this before.

So with a tear in his eye he told him that his only sister was dying in Ipswich and he just wanted to see her before she rolled over and that they were very close since mum and dad died. And he just stared at me and blinked a couple of times, then grabbed my gear, laptop and carry-on shit and practically ran me to the plane, he thought he would have seated him if they would have let him. He thanked him profusely and he gave him the don't mention it Bud thing, and was gone. Jim was a pretty good bullshitter when he had to be but he tended to outdo himself sometimes, he guessed this time he excelled.

But here he was reading the paper and getting airborne, if that guy at security had as many air hours as him he would have likely had wings. Shit he hated using people like that. He arrived in Vancouver with fifteen minutes to boarding time, he did it right, no bells and whistles, just slipped on through and he was almost asleep before takeoff. He came to with this ugly stewardess shaking the hell out of him, he guessed she thought he was dead, they were fifteen minutes to Heathrow. Not bad, missed supper and breakfast, hadn't eaten since yesterday morning at the Frontier.

He cabbed it to the Metropolitan, just off Leicester Square, a middle-of-the-line price for London. By Vancouver Chamber of Commerce standards they would consider it a fucking slum, you took one look at the staff and you figured you were in Bangladesh, hey that's OK, he was only sleeping there. He made the call using his best Cockney accent.

"What's up then, I owe you one mate, how about the Strand?"

All he got back was:

"Right!"

Then a hang-up. All was well, they had five hotels they used and each one meant someplace else and it also meant eight thirty am. The Strand was a twenty-four hour greasy spoon on the M1, about five acres of transport trucks or better known in Blighty as lorries, heading in all directions. This shack would be bulldozed over on the I.5, but the food was great, well depending on what you were used to, that is. Jim was ex-military, so it was great.

Now he headed next door from the Met, to the Jack and Lion, and had a pub meal and a warm pint or two. The cod was hanging over each end of the plate and the chips were stacked high (French fries in US and Canada). London chips with malt vinegar and don't dare ask for ketchup. You could take your fork and place it on the fish and press it down and watch the grease ooze out of it, his kind of nosh, he was drooling, but not for long.

He got into that like it was the Last Supper, and guess what? You could smoke in the bar (illegally), so he did that as well. One more pint then back to his room, checked his mail, then hit the sack.

Six-thirty he was on the M1 with his thumb out, Doc Martens boots, blue jeans, an over-the-ass black duffle jacket with the collar up and a black toque. Fifteen minutes and he had his ride, heading for Newcastle and he dropped him at the long hauler by eight.

The Commander would leave his home and go straight to his office at six-thirty am every day, this morning he parked at his lot and walked straight in as usual, straight in through the front door, but instead of going upstairs he headed out through the back, across the alley and through the back door of the bakery and out the front and a small Morris Minor was waiting for him.

He wasted no time and headed around a maze of alleys and back streets, then hit the M1 and made time, till he was bouncing through the potholes at the long hauler and parked at the front, in a spot reserved for non-truckers. He grabbed his briefcase and plopped on his bowler and headed in through the front door, top coat flapping open, showing a dark pin striped three-piece, with a regimental tie, his moustache was waxed at the ends and pointing at a nice forty-five degree angle, shoes shining. Old warrior written all over him, he spotted his target at the back and headed that way, getting some funny looks from the clientele.

One old driver piped up, "Hey Guvnor, made the wrong turn then?"

He turned back and shouted:

"Not at all mate, the missus told me to meet her at the best place in town. Don't know where she got to, but I'm here, right?"

There was a good round of laughter and some clapping. He dropped his briefcase in the booth and pulled off his top coat and slid in, sticking out his hand.

"Good to see you Jim, looks like life is treating you well."

"It is too Commander, you don't look like you are hurting any."

"Not a damned bit lad. One thing though, they gave me a little Morris Minor this time and I could hardly get in to it, stupid buggers, I'm six three, I nearly had an accident just trying to manoeuver that little thing around." The commander took his slinking around very seriously, although he loved the games he played.

Obscurity to the trade had kept him in business a long time and his clients liked it as well, his contractors as he called them, insisted on it. A known face was a lost cause, grounds for an early retirement.

"Let's order and get some nosh inside us, then get the old heartburn going."

They both ordered the eighteen-wheel special from a waitress pushing forty and still thinking she was twenty and dressed the same way.

"More char love?"

"Thanks love."

"And you Guvnor, have a top up?"

"Yes I will, thanks love."

She gave the bowler hat a look.

"Don't see many of them in here then, looks like you've had it a bit then.

"Suits you with that waxed mouser an' all, bet you were in the Guards or summink like that then."

"Well, something like that."

"Oh, a bit hush, hush then?"

"Not really, just doing our bit you know."

"I'll bet you were, love. I'll just get your order then and get things moving."

And she wiggled away to the counter.

"All right Jim, I'll just slip you the file."

And he opened his case and pulled out a large manila envelope and passed it over.

"You can look at that later, I'll just talk about it right now and let you know what I've gleaned from around the table, from the boys in low places. There are maps in there and locations marked, it's going to be expensive, lots of travel, the usual stuff. I've accepted it only on the condition that you and your team take it on, it doesn't need the hardcore type, like some of the other lads I have on my books. They're bloody brutal, but I won't push you, just let me know by tonight."

And with that the food arrived. Two big platters the size of hub caps laden with food: eggs, bacon, fried bread with stewed tomatoes and beans on top, I don't know why they call it lorry drivers' food, you could find it in any mess hall in the British army, I suppose half the drivers did their bit for their country anyway.

So they bowed their heads and did it justice and stuck in, a bit of a squirt of the HP sauce that sat on every table.

Once this was cleared away they pushed the plates back and stepped to the back door, to the smokers' table, just outside. Reaching for his smokes he passed his pack to the Commander.

"Not on your nelly Jim, can't abide those Yank fags, not after a nosh up like that."

The Commander pulled a pack of Capstan full strength from a vest pocket and as he laid them on the table and wrinkled his nose at the smell of the Marlboro, a head turned round,

"Hey mate, those Yank fags then? Let's have one then," and he threw the pack over, got it back with a big smile.

"Where did you get them then mate?"

"At the docks."

"Ah going there for my next load, might get lucky myself then.

"Hey need a ride then?"

" Wouldn't mind at all."

"Well I leave on five."

"You're on, thanks mate."

"Ok Commander I'll let you know tonight, I'll give you the wrong number routine if I'm in, I'll just hang up if I'm not."

"Thanks Jim, hope you take it." And Jim left with his new trucker mate, heading back to London.

The commander leant on the smokers' table and pulled out a Capstan Plain and started feeling for the matches he didn't have. A pack of Puck landed on the table and he looked up at an old trucker just across the way.

"Can't bear to watch a serious smoker suffer mate," and he gave the Commander a smile.

"Thanks lad, you saved the day," and he lit up and threw the matches and the smokes back.

"Can't get caught with them in my pocket, the missus would have a fit, so enjoy."

"Thanks Mate."

"Don't know what those young lads see in those Yank fags."

"Ah, it's just a bloody fad, there is nothing in them, you no sooner have one and you're looking for another, I think that's the idea."

"Aye you're right, now on the other hand, one of these and you're good for a while, right?"

And he disappeared behind a cloud of blue smoke, with a big smile. He left a handsome tip and headed out to the Morris, 'hope the blighter takes the job, best one I've got for it. I just know he will,' and he headed back to London by another route.

They chatted and smoked all the way to the docks and then he bailed, leaving the pack, just in case.

He said "Thanks mate" and wheeled away in a cloud of diesel smoke. He grabbed a cab and was back in his room just as a light rain started. He threw his coat on the chair and propped himself up on the bed and spread out the pictures and maps and read the breakdown again from end-to-end. He leaned back on the headboard and thought it out. This guy was going to walk with two murders, not right, someone should give him a little smack on his pe pe and it might as well be him. He grabbed his cell and dialled the Commander's number and caught him still on the road.

"Hello!"

"Who is this then?"

"If you don't know mate then you must have the wrong number, right?"

"That's it! I've got the wrong number, shithead," and he hung up and chuckled to himself. 'Old bugger!'

He chuckled again and rubbed his hands together, 'good on you Jimmy my boy, now I don't have to worry do I?'

In the hotel he slipped on his jacket and went for a stroll in the rain, found a payphone and made a rather long, detailed call to a construction company in Scotland. Signed off, then arranged a flight to Boston for the following morning, had an early supper and went for a pint, just to remind him why he left Blighty in the first place, the rain and the warm beer, he didn't think any of those pubs had heard of cold beer. He was on the go at three-thirty for a six am flight and did it all right again, without a rushed breakfast at thirty thousand feet, then headed down to Logan International and arrived on time, it was a fresh but sunny day, he guessed fall was in the air. Got a hotel close to where he wanted to be, a little more pricey, but a lot better service. Sent out his cleaning and laundry and had it back by noon, got a cheap pair of binos and staked out his project.

She arrived at three-thirty and the staff started to leave around five, the last two guys left together at five thirty-five. He was crossing the parking lot when the old guy came out, the caretaker and he walked right past and up the ally never looking back. Ed didn't even notice. He doubled back and with a credit card slipped the lock and he was in.

CHAPTER 8

SHE WAS AT HER DESK AND IT WAS CUT AND PASTE TIME, for the stories from different parts of the universe were in for the printing, and she wouldn't allow anything on paper that she hadn't read and approved. Everyone tried to get the most mileage out of their story; it's just human nature, so she cut till all the pages were filled with the best there was, no filler, like loose jargon that said nothing, not in this mag. Suddenly she jumped as the chair across from her creaked. The office was in darkness, just monitor lights glowing and there was some guy sitting in that chair.

"Mrs. Lawrence, hope I didn't startle you."

She was scared, this had never happened before.

"How did you get in here?" she asked, and he just pointed at the door. She was sure Les closed up when leaving, where did this guy come from? So she tried to play it cool. Is this one of those weirdo-like molesters? Shit, she always planned on getting a gun, why hadn't she? It didn't fit, he was sitting, lighting a cigarette, for God's sake. 'OK, I've got to handle this.'

"Well what can I do for you? If it's a job you are after, I don't know if we need anyone right now."

"Well I was under the impression you did," and the smoke just curled up through the light from the desk lamp, and it hit home like a hammer and she almost jumped.

"I believe you contacted a friend of a friend."

"Yes! Yes, I did, I'm sorry, it just didn't click."

"All I want to do is ask you a few questions, like do you still want to go through with this, and I want to hear you say it."

She tried to get a better look at this guy, a good six feet and some, a good sun tan likely from all the other places he has been doing things for other folks. He had on blue jeans with razor sharp creases and western boots and a sports coat with a black shirt, couldn't see any more.

"Well, do you or don't you?"

And she almost shouted:

"You're damned right I do."

"That's what I wanted to hear from you."

He reached inside his sports coat and took out an envelope and passed it over to her.

"Take a look and tell me if you have ever seen that male before."

She fumbled with the tab and pulled out a picture of a couple, a young man with his arm draped around a good looking girl and looking sure of himself, in an arrogant kind of way, very snappy dresser, white suit, good tan, dark hair, well groomed.

"No, I've never seen him before, I'm sure of it."

There was a slight pause and he said,

"That's the man who killed your daughter and Lisa Thornton."

She jumped out of the chair and grabbed a napkin from a box on the desk and was violently sick, it ran over her hands and she grabbed more and cleaned herself, wiping her lips and trembling violently.

"That was taken the night before the hit and run. Your daughter was dead by this time."

"How do you know he is guilty? Scotland Yard gave him a clean bill of health," and he just looked at her.

"Yes I know they did, but they had to. They have to deal with facts, and proof whereas I don't."

"Oh, you're just going to walk up to him and ask him if he murdered two people?"

"Close."

She didn't know how to react to this statement.

"Pretty close!"

"Exactly what do you mean, pretty close?"

"Mrs. Lawrence, you don't need to know all the details. But if he did the crime, I can almost guarantee he will say so, and we are not going to beat it out of him, but unlike Scotland Yard, we will get it out of him, then pass it on to you as proof, before you commit yourself. As you know, he is just part of the problem. If you accept our proof, we will carry the punishment far beyond Oxford."

"Yes you are right, it is not just him that is the problem, although he is the one that killed my daughter."

"Yes he is."

"What would you do in order to carry out this punishment, as you call it?"

"We would go to Panama and put the family out of business or out of existence. Mrs. Lawrence, I've said too much as it is, if you get questioned by the authorities and you know nothing, what can you tell them? Nothing, so I will say no more, except in a few days you will have your evidence and we will expect your answer. If it is yes you, will deposit a check for 300,000 US dollars in the account number given to you at the time, and a check for 200,000 on completion. Expenses will be over and above that and they could go to 100,000."

"Wow I didn't know you could make money that fast, that easy."

"People are going to lose their lives I hope, theirs not mine. Two people have already been killed, that should never have happened. When I send you my report, then you can make your decision, if the money is deposited I will take that as an accept and I will proceed. Once that starts, there is no stopping it, if the money is not deposited, then I will take that as a no-go and you will never see or hear from me again."

When she looked up, he was closing the door behind him, just as silently as when he came in and he was gone. She was trembling, 'what have I done? God, what have I got myself into? Well I've still got a way out.'

It's just not what she expected. She was looking for a GI Joe type, combat boots with a Stallone or Arnie face, she didn't expect a junior gentleman.

When he left the building he took out a cell and made a call using a calling card and waited. When it was answered all he said was:

"Do it." then hung up.

He caught a cab and went for a ride, once they hit traffic he dropped the cell from the window and watched the evening commuters take their toll. He left the cab in .

the heart of town, walked a short distance on Harlequin to a small restaurant he ate, and killed some time, then took another cab back to Logan international. He caught an evening flight with KLM, which would put him in Amsterdam for breakfast. Then the wait.

Amsterdam, because it is a neutral city, no-one gave a shit, pawn shops sold cells by the handful, still working, every bar had a display of joints on the counter, you just pointed and you got, hookers were ten-a-penny, the cops would help you get whatever you wanted for a price. And any name is good enough, Jim had a passport that he had had for three years and as a matter of fact he got it there. His picture, but another name, he didn't go into that, it just showed that Robin Taylor was in Amsterdam today and that Jim Cowan had never left Canada, maybe still fishing in Kinbasket Lake, not really necessary but just to be on the safe side. Anything could go wrong with the next little move and he didn't want to be close. His rock ape friends in Scotland were good, but sometimes a little rough around the edges, with your back against the wall and the bullets flying there weren't any better troops out there, none by his book.

But this little project they were going to tackle for him was delicate; he knew Bob could handle it, but his brothers were kind of rogues and needed a little guidance, which Bobbie would hand out with a vicious streak, that Jim thought he would enjoy. He never took anything on that he wasn't in charge of and that he respected. If anything went wrong, it wouldn't matter what, it never came back to you, never! And he'd given him the go ahead, now it was wait time for him, the hardest part of all.

So he had something to eat, a beer and whatever Amsterdam had to throw at him, in a pleasant sort of way, that is.

CHAPTER 9

THE OLDER BLACK THAMES TRADER VAN JUST LEFT THE M1 an hour ago and was parked just down the street from the Gloucester Hotel. There was lots of room in the parking lot but sometimes hotels had surveillance, kept an eye on parking lots. The next time a customer did a bunk on them would be the last, each spot would have a number, not on the lot, but on the wall behind reception and keys would be hanging on that spot for that vehicle. Now if the valet was sitting sipping tea and that vehicle started to move they could be on it immediately, so better park somewhere else. They had plates from another vehicle that they had just scrounged, not as easy in the UK as in the US or Canada - in the UK the vehicle left the dealer with the plates on it and they stayed there till it went to the boneyard, so usually it just wasn't a couple of screws, maybe four or six and sometimes rectangular or square plates depending on the vehicle, so a little more caution was in demand. A plate from a Ford would not be the plate you'd see on a Beamer. Anyway it was dark and they would be off before light.

2.30am three figures left the parking spot and walked off, one carrying a suitcase, medium size, just right for carry-on luggage, no bigger, they walked along casually and with a glance behind took the alley to the rear of the hotel. The fire escape ladder was approximately twelve feet above their heads, black leather gloves were slipped on, then the larger of the three braced his hands on the wall, the medium-sized one held his hands with his fingers woven together and did a lift of the shorter, lighter one and practically threw him onto the larger one's shoulders.

He no sooner landed there than he started to feed the ladder down, which was grabbed by Number Two. They both scrambled up it, after throwing the suitcase up to the light one, and then the ladder was stored back in its place.

This took less than thirty seconds, the room they were looking for was on the second floor and the window was right in front of them, which looked right down the hallway to a fella slouched in a chair, sound asleep, they hoped! The window was an older vertical lift with a simple swing latch, the switch blade was thrust between the two parts and the latch swung back easily. The larger one took out a Glock 9-mil with a large suppressor on it and entered the hallway, first he pointed it at the sleeping form and started to advance towards him, the second two opened the case and removed a Ziploc bag with a large white pad in it. They removed the pad and advanced, with their older brother. The sleeper in the chair didn't stand a chance, one grabbed him in a bear hug, chair and all, the pistol was thrust against his forehead and the pad placed over his mouth and nose and was held firm in place for ten seconds or till he had a couple of good breaths. He was laid on the floor with his chair, this was a large man, the leather gloves were removed and replaced with latex, two more pads were removed, dripping with ethyl chloride, the door was slowly opened and all moved inside, leaving the sleeping form in the hallway.

The room was in darkness, only the neon lights from the street below showed through the large window, which was enough. Moving swiftly and efficiently it was over in seconds, two of them left for the hallway and the outside guard was dragged in. Martinez was dragged from the bed and the guard was stripped and lifted in to the bed, a used condom was roughly pulled into place, then both bodies were wrapped around each other. All Martinez's clothes were gathered and placed in the small suitcase they brought, the guard's clothes were then spread around the room, a shoulder holster was taken and draped over the bedpost with a revolver in it, a clear plastic tube was then slid down his throat and a small funnel attached and three-quarters of a bottle of Scotch was poured into him. Lines of coke were laid out on the glass coffee table, then half-blown away, a rolled up five-pound note placed in the guard's hand then with a Q-tip the white powder was dabbed around both their noses, the big man nodded and smiled. Martinez was then rolled in a blanket that they had brought and slung over the middle man's shoulder, the youngest of the three then left by the fire escape, the second started down the hallway, avoiding the elevator and took the stairwell, with a well-placed sticker on his rump that said Stag Lad. The senior of the three then went around the room and touched it up and left after his brother, just closing the door but not tight so one push would open it.

The stairwell door opened into the alley and the black van was idling there with the sliding door on the side open. The one carrying the body went straight inside and the older brother closed it without slamming it. Then he jumped into the front passenger seat and the van moved away. He looked at his watch, smiled and spoke for the first time.

"Twenty minutes from start to finish, not bad lads, not bad at all."

They headed in the direction of the motorway, John the oldest said:

"Pull over here, at the payphone," which he did. John then opened the door and punched in 999. The British police number all over the island, 999; it was answered by a dispatcher, who after some persuasion put him through to the local police:

"High Wycombe Constabulary, Constable Sinclair speaking, how may I help you?"

And with his best Cockney tongue he answered.

"Want to make a little cocaine bust this morning? Help start your day off right."

And he gave the hotel and the room.

"Do it quiet like and you could catch the lot."

And he hung up, got back in the van and pulled away, heading for the M1 and north.

Before the sliproad a police car passed them, going the other way, with all the lights on and no ding dongs.

"Wonder where he is off to then," the driver said.

"Stumps, I sometimes wonder, the two days you went

to school, were you sleeping? God what did I do to earn that then? Never mind, Jack give his lordship a shot of propofol, that should hold him for some time, save any trouble, then get the straitjacket on him and the leg cuffs, then cover him up like a good lad."

"Hey Johnny, are we going to stop for something to eat, I'm starving?"

"Aye well, let's get up the road a bit first, then we can find one of those all night diners," they were back in their native Glasgow tongue and enjoying their success of a job well done. John glanced at the speedometer then looked at his younger brother and shook his head.

"Stumps, if we get stopped for a speeding ticket I'll break your fucking neck, then work my way down your body breaking what's left, and I guarantee it won't be nice," and there was a sudden decrease in speed. By mid-morning they were crossing the border into Scotland and almost home.

Propped up on his bed trying to read a Dutch paper and catching enough to get the gist of it; these little countries take their politics seriously, even half their funnies are political but still funny, Jim's eye just caught the laptop's wink. He had mail, he crossed his fingers and dragged his carcass to the end of the bed where he used the bed for his chair and brought the PC around to face him and tap the appropriate buttons.

It read: 'First phase of project complete, second

phase should be completed in twenty-four hours, will expect payment for renovation project on completion of third phase, satisfaction guaranteed.' Great, that was the iffy part, but it looked like it went well. During which time he placed a pending order to the Commander. He'd formed a sketchy plan and the equipment needed if all was go, some of the gear might take a little time to put together so it was just heads up. He was starting to get a little excited, something he tried to avoid as that was when things got all loose and they couldn't afford that, so he tried to button it down and stay cool.

The next twenty four hours took twenty-four hours and he counted the minutes, it was a long time, he wasn't good at this part, especially relying on someone else. It was early evening, he'd had a nice big meal, trying to kill time he'd walked to the hotel, again trying to kill time, now he was crossing the lobby and the bellhop grabbed his arm, he almost dropped him when he realized he was calling him Taylor and the two receptionists were doing the same thing. Taylor was the name on his bogus passport, he was so absorbed with his waiting time he just for a moment forgot, he never thought, very bad on his part and he apologized profusely and told them about his hearing problem and he got the sad look of pity. Then she held up a small package, 'for you Mr Taylor' for which he thanked her profusely, signed for the package and tipped handsomely, then scurried up to his room with it.

Wow, it was from his mum, smart buggers, this package had been opened. Not a big deal, what with bombing and terrorism, what could you expect? The tape reapplied over the opening then customs-sealed, he cut it all away, inside was a note from his mum, quite remarkable considering she's been dead for the past five years, anyway the note read:

'My loving son, you left home without your music and I know how you can't live without it, and how your father can't live with it, but not to worry. Mum took care of it and I'll get a nice big hug when you get back. Now don't you be going and eating any of that strange food you get over there, you know how your stomach acts up. All my love, Mum.'

Those guys could not do a job without making a bit of a joke about it. They never could.

Inside, a mountain of tissue paper and wrapped till he thought he would never get to it, was an ipod with a set of earphones. He stuck them in and turned on, and the heavy metal that came out you would have thought the band was in his room, non-stop, he rewound it and then skipped ahead twenty songs, then pressed the play and caught the end of a song that should never have been recorded, then silence. This Scottish voice came on and he listened to it, all good stuff. This would bring an answer real fast and he'd be very surprised if it was negative. He folded all the wrapping into the trash and mum's note.

Phoned and got an 8am flight on KLM for Boston, best he could do. Then to a bank in Ireland and made a transfer to a bank in Cyprus of five thousand pounds. Most of the regiment guys liked Cyprus as they did a lot of time on the island, they had three airbases there and did a lot of chopper work out of Cyprus, some other things as well. Anyway, a lot of guys had offshore accounts in

Cyprus, Jim included, but he liked to spread it around just in case of any mishap. Not that he had a lot to spread around, but may as well keep them guessing.

So, would arrive around eight-thirty Saturday evening and that is what he did. There's a UPS right across from Logan and that was his first stop, he wrote a little note and shoved it inside a bubble-wrapped envelope along with the ipod and earpieces, the note just told her to scroll through twenty pieces before listening, a kind of standard number for them. Seal it up, paid his thirty bucks and watched the courier head out with it to his minivan, guess he just got in under the wire. Back at the hotel, a shower and a shave, laundry in the bag, filled out the little list they required, how many pairs of shorts, do you want starch on your collars, they didn't miss much. He gave them a call and told them it was urgent and the hop was there before he'd got it all ready. Love good service. He tried to give it, and he liked to get it. He phoned room service and ordered off the in-house menu, along with a six-pack and sat around with a towel wrapped around him watching the Shark Tank, waiting for his clothes, and food. The food came first and he was starving and made short work of it, and he chugalugged two beers while he ate. He had given the UPS people her phone number and they phoned ahead with a delivery time, within the hour. He set up his laptop with his Cyprus account on-line and had another beer.

CHAPTER 10

SHE WAS SITTING AROUND IN SWEATS AND FLIP FLOPS watching TV when the phone rang and she reached for it without taking her eyes off the set. UPS got a delivery within the hour.

"Fine, I'll be here," and hung up. She started surfing through the channels and stopped at the Shark Tank and started to watch, not thinking about the delivery, had a good idea it was a piece from an overseas reporter, one of the projects over there was heating up so she would look at it, when it came in. Edit it and take it in in the morning. Save some time.

So the ding dong wasn't a surprise and she went through with a five in her hand, signed and took the little padded envelope and wandered back to the front of the TV. This wasn't what she had been expecting, quite heavy for its size, she slipped her finger under the sticky tab and opened it. First she pulled out the note written in ballpoint and started to read, suddenly she realized this wasn't what she expected, and rose and went into her office, laid the note on the desk and dumped the envelope on the blotter, picked up the ipod and read the note again.

Then realization came to her and she fumbled with the little earpieces finally getting them in, she switched it on and was startled with the blast and rolled the volume down, then looked at the note again and started to count ahead, the twentieth song ended, then there was silence and a slight hiss as it moved on, then a man's voice with a strong accent started to speak, Irish or a Scot yes definitely Scot and she listened intently.

"This is an informal interrogation. Now I want you to speak into the mike clearly please and answer all the questions to the best of your ability, yes?"

"No."

"With no idle chatter, got it?"

"Fuck off, and hiding behind those stupid masks won't get you off the hook."

"Just answer the questions. What is your name?"

She almost answered when she realised he wasn't speaking to her.

"Well if you don't know that my friend, you are in deep shit. Well you are in deep shit, but I'll play your little game any way, as you will have to play mine in the end, and that will be an experience you will remember till the end of your fucking miserable life anyway.

"Answer the fucking question," and the slap could be heard quite clearly and unmistakably.

"I'll ask, you will answer just what I ask, got it?" There was a slight pause and a more subdued answer.

"My name is Louis Eduardo Martinez."

"Where is your homeland?"

"Panama."

"Where in Panama?"

"Panama City."

"Who is your father?"

"My father is Gerardo Moncado Martinez and you will find out soon e..." and another slap could be heard quite clearly.

"Are you Latinos slow or something? I ask, you answer. Why are you here?"

"I'm a student at the University of Oxford."

"Oh, do you like that? You throw the odd, party invite a good crowd?"

"Sometimes, for my friends."

"Any drugs?"

"Not to my knowledge."

"Enough of this bullshit, take him out, oh here, shoot him up and bring him back in fifteen."

"Don't do this, it would be very stupid of you."

"Take him out."

"You bastardos will pay with your fucking lives, I will personally see to it."

"Get him out I said and if he fucks you around, slap him, got it?"

And the sound of a scuffle and some dragging, then door slamming and muffled screaming. Then that strong Scottish voice was back again.

"Sorry for the delay, we are going to administer a talker, a truth serum, he is going to sound a little sleepy and slurry, but it removes all inhibitions and they talk more freely, and relaxed."

The recording seemed to stop and start again, this time the attitude was different.

"Your name please?"

And the whole procedure was gone through again. Yes, sleepy and definitely slurring a little but you could tell it was the same person.

"You threw parties?"

"Yes."

"You supplied the food?"

"Yes."

"The booze?"

"Yes."

"Hookers?"

"Yes."

"Drugs?"

"Yes."

"You killed the Lawrence girl?"

"No."

"You gave her drugs?"

"She wouldn't take them."

"What's them?"

"Cocaine, ecstasy. She wouldn't take nothing!"

"How come she died then?"

"We gave it to her."

"You forced her?"

"Yes."

"How do you force someone?"

"Same way every time, you hold them face down, blindfold them, tape their mouth and close one nostril, they got to suck it up, then close the other nostril and do it again, if you feel like it."

"You did that to the Lawrence girl?"

"Yes."

"How many times?"

"Don't know, too many times I guess," and he snickered.

"Fucking bitch!"

"So you killed her?"

"No, that wasn't meant to happen."

"What was meant to happen, and why?"

"Why? She rejected me, fucking slut, I sent her a limo, flowers, shit, everything and she wouldn't even give me the time of day. So I thought I'd loosen her up a bit and got the guys to do her over."

"Then she died, right?

"So you killed her?"

"Well I guess so, stuck up Yank bitch, we sell more drugs in the good old US of A than anywhere else, so what's the problem?"

"The problem is, you killed someone."

"Well if that is what this is all about, give me a name, we will send them some bucks, that cures all don't it," another snicker.

"OK, what about the other girl?"

"What other girl?" And you could hear the papers getting sorted out and a whisper.

"Better get on with it lad, this won't hold for ever, right, OK, Lisa Thornton, that one."

"What about her?"

"I asked, did you kill her?"

"It was arranged."

"Why?"

"She talked too much."

"What do you mean, too much?"

"Well, to the wrong people."

"Who, the bobbies?"

"No, we don't worry about the bobbies."

"Who did she talk to then?"

"The Lawrence woman, that's who."

"What about?"

"About me and she had been warned, but wouldn't listen."

"So you had her removed."

"Right."

"What about the Lawrence woman then?"

"My father brought me home for a while, said it would go away."

"Did it?"

"Yes, she left, and we haven't heard from her since."

"Who is we?"

"My father has some big shot in the police force that keeps him clued in."

"The Inspector?"

"No, a big shot, I don't know who."

"OK guys, I've got all I want, get this piece of shit out of here, give him a shower, feed him then back in the cage, cuffs on at all times and only one doing and one watching, got it?"

"Don't worry, we know the drill."

"Good." It went dead, then the music started again and she shut it off.

She wanted to play it again but couldn't because she was trembling uncontrollably and silently sobbing, thinking what her daughter must have gone through before she died. 'Those sons of bitches killed my little girl, they took away my world, and the cops can do nothing! Not a fucking thing! Nothing! Money covers all, well you bastards, I've got a few bucks myself, let's see what they can do for me and I hope it makes your life fucking miserable.' She made a transfer to a bank in Cyprus and watched it go through. 'Go get those bastards and do it right. Oh God forgive me, but do it right!'

CHAPTER 11

THE WINK ON THE PC WASN'T MISSED AND HE PRESSED one key and the account in Cyprus popped up, with an incoming figure and a transfer to another in the Cayman Islands. He didn't think it would take long, but didn't think it would be this soon either. Well, it's time to go to work so he made a call to Logan and arranged an evening flight to LAX, then a call to Liverpool, England one more to Huntingdon Beach, closed up all his gear and was ready to go. His flight to LA broke at Dallas for one hour, he was in LA by three-thirty. He opened a cell and made a call, the chirping took three chirps and was answered with a strong deep voice

"Your dime so use the line, buddy."

"Surf is up Dude, see you at six."

"You got it," and the call was over. He was booked for one night at the Huntingdon Hyatt and he got a rental for the next morning. He needed it at 5.30am and so it was confirmed.

He was tired and a little wired. After checking in he grabbed a Bud from the minibar and walked out on to the balcony to watch the sun going down. It only took ten minutes and was gone. He finished his smoke and beer and headed for the dining room, an early supper and then an email to a contractor in Scotland, thanking him for the fine job, and the approval for the next phase had been approved, and to please proceed with great haste as time was of the essence. The team was hoping for a four-day completion, this caused a disruption at the other end.

The three brothers prepared to visit their prisoner at the storage yard, it was an evening call so the dogs would be on the loose and allowed to wander while they were in the yard. After they entered the compound and the gates re-closed, the dogs were released again; they were big animals, but not half as vicious as they looked, so did a very good job. They parked their van at the rear of the house so it was invisible from the street.

The property was five acres and full of piles of lumber and parked equipment and an extra vehicle would surely be unnoticed. No-one but the brothers were allowed in the yard after five-thirty, not with the animals on the loose, they told everyone it wouldn't be safe. They entered the house through the back door and descended to the basement, flicked on the lights and opened the cell and their project was lying on his back on a bunk and didn't move. Their masks were in place, he would likely never see them again, but no chances were taken.

He was blindfolded and strapped onto the bench that was his bed, secured by wide padded straps, legs, arms, waist and head completely immobile. Then, from a back room an apparatus like an IV stand was brought out and from a briefcase, a bag containing a saline solution with cocaine mix was brought in to play. His immobile arm was slapped and swabbed and an IV slipped in to the main artery, the body was vibrating and the older brother talked to him.

"You are being fed by IV, so you get all the nutrition you need so don't worry, it's not going away so relax and enjoy the ride," and he smiled at his brothers and walked out with them both behind him. When in the outer room with the door closed he gave his instructions.

"This lad will never be left alone, not for the first two days anyway, not till we find his strengths, we are not going to kill him, but we are really going to fuck him up big time, in fact he will never be the same again. We have limited time to do this little feat, our man wants it sewn up within the week, not a problem, but I don't want him dead Capish? So all he can take, but alive. If by any chance he dies on me, I say me because I'm responsible, you boys decide which one wants to take his place, and that will be the lucky one," and he left his two brothers looking at each other with worried expressions on their faces, and they both darted back into the room to check on their charge.

These two young men were fearless, any fight was good enough, if John said take that guy out he was as good as dead, but their one fear was their brother who they loved unconditionally, John had spent two years in the Gordon Highlanders, seven in the SAS, Britain's undisputed finest, then he had worked for Jim for five doing whatever he asked him to do, till he had enough money to start the building business, rescuing his youngest brother from jail, the other from a life of drugs and crime before he went to jail. Business was good, they built Glasgow's finest homes and had a crew of at least three hundred fine tradesmen on the payroll, they had nice homes and drove good cars and John got his start with James and has never forgotten it and wouldn't let them forget it either.

CHAPTER 12

FIVE-THIRTY FOUND HIM ON THE 405 AND ALMOST AT HIS destination, he lit a smoke to enjoy before he got there, smoking in California was like doing drugs on the street. You would draw less attention walking naked than you would smoking, a cig in your hand was like being a leper! So he sucked it back as he pulled in to the IHop on Beach Boulevard and Pacific Coast Highway and slid into a parking spot on a nearly-empty lot. A little early for the average beach bum, he got out and dropped his butt and screwed it out, looked around and kicked it under his car, and shook his head, 'CA does that to me.'

He walked across the parking lot that was just starting to heat up, by ten you would never make it on your bare feet. He shoved open the double glass doors and was met by a blast of cold air already blowing through the place. He selected a booth looking out on the parking lot and plopped down and ordered a coffee from a waitress in a sweater, and saw the big black pickup come squealing into the lot and angle park across two spots. Nothing like being inconspicuous, and told the girl, better make that two then two big breakfasts to follow. 'You got it.' and she wiggled off to the ordering tablet.

Chuck was six-two, blond curly hair hanging over his brow and with a tan that would make the average sun seeker say, 'he must be local.' Torn blue jeans cut off at the knees and tattered with too many washes and bleached almost white, a Hawaiian shirt open down the front with more colours than an African parrot, at least a five day growth on his blond beard. And this was my right hand man. One of the best soldiers I have ever came across, he hailed from Texas and didn't have a living soul in that state he could call family, right off the ranch, first Lieutenant in the navy two years, five years Navy Seals, good people, solid as a rock.

He slid in to the booth opposite Jim and stuck his hand out. He gave it a squeeze and they both smiled.

"Well, got something good for us?"

"I think so," and he slid over the file with most of the stuff he got from the Commander, Chuck looked over his shoulder and pulled it out, sat back and started to read between slurps of coffee. He read it right through and nodded his head.

"Count me in and I'll call Pedro, he will want a piece of this, is that OK?"

"Absolutely, we must have Pedro, he is the only one that could pass for a Panamanian."

"Who else do you have in mind?"

"OJ wants a piece, spending more money on that club, and those three kids of his, nothing but the best for them. For a tough guy he is a pushover really, born and raised in Detroit but thinks Liverpool is the capital of the world. I would say his heritage is Jamaican and his wife Maxine is as blond as Goldie Hawn, dresses like a hooker and has the mind of a New York stockbroker, handles all the books for two clubs and three kids at the same time. I wouldn't say the odd couple, but OJ is six three, Maxine might make five two with those really high heels and they love each other unconditionally."

Jim met OJ while on detachment in Yemen, they were attached to the 45 Commando Royal Marines, OJ was a sergeant with them, he didn't like him at first, he thought he was pretending to be an American, he didn't realize at the time, he was.

"We became really good friends while over there, after I found out he was from Detroit.

"His father was a Vietnam vet and his mother had passed on, he couldn't get in the US Marines because of a record so went to Blighty and told them he wanted to be a Marine, and the man said let's see if you are good enough, he did nine years.

"Met Maxine in a bar in Liverpool, beat the shit out of her one-night-stand and told her 'no more messin' around woman, you're with me now, so show some respect, what are our kids going to say?"

"What kids?" she said.

"Well the ones we are going to have after you marry me."

"Well Sunshine, is that a proposal or something?"

"What's the matter woman, are you slow or somethin'? Of course it is. What do you say? We going to do it or not?"

"And they were married two weeks later and lived like best friends and true lovers ever since. Maxine had run that club for a couple of gay guys, until OJ bought it for her. The couple couldn't get along any more and OJ made them an offer and they jumped at it to get out.

"OJ is good solid stuff, I like working with him."

"Is that it then?"

"At this point I don't think we need any more, if it gets complicated we might pick up a couple more, but for now, that's it, we will leave from Mexico, meet at Pedro's. I'll pick up OJ from LAX, and we will head south to Pedro's, then drive to La Paz and take the ferry to Mazatlan, catch a shuttle to Acapulco, there is a vehicle there with a driver to take us to a strip outside Oaxaca, then go in high with a night-drop, two days recon, then do it, and out."

"Sounds good to me," and the waitress arrived with the platters of food and they ate and drank coffee and hashed out some of the smaller details.

Chuck, his number two would slide in to number one place if anything happened to him so he had to be filled in on all the details: the Scottish raiding party and how long it would take to complete, as that was crucial to their plan. The lad would be taken back to Panama as fast as possible and into the mountains, where his family had a mansion, hidden in the jungle. Also where the cocaine was finished and packed and shipped to different locations for distribution, there were laboratories built out of concrete blocks, where all the testing, they assumed, was done. Three long warehouses, each approximately one hundred feet by forty, there was no way you could see inside them, but a real reconnaissance from the Commander showed those buildings were full of people working. Large nets hung over everything except the house and this was approximately one hundred yards away from everything else. A short mile down there was an airstrip and at the home, a helipad. No road in or out for a vehicle, the workers would walk in on trails and once in would stay for a duration of time, but no access for a vehicle.

This is where they would take junior to recuperate he hoped, then fly in a doctor. And this was where he wanted to hit them, after this there would be no more Martinezes, and no more business, he hoped. The guards were in the region of fifteen or twenty, minimum five on shift day or night. The guards even had their own pool separate from the family, very relaxed.

This establishment had never been hit by anyone, DEA or the Panamanian authorities, this was a no-no place to go. That could cut El Presidente's check in half.

They were going to cause a political disaster, but they didn't give a shit as long as they couldn't trace it back to them. The DEA, CIA, and a number of outside authorities were going to feel the heat. There was still some last minute stuff to sort out, and Chuck would be the first to know.

Weaponry would be handled by the Commander, all he had to do was let him know what he wanted. Make, brand or model didn't matter as long as they were in good working order, and he had a plan going on in his head, so they shook hands and he left, he wouldn't see Chuck till Pedro's, and they would travel separately, Chuck to Pedro's, OJ and Jim from LAX. He would buy an older pick-up with CA plates and he had another passport and ID for OJ, so when he arrived in L.A. he'd never left the

US till time to go home, they would head south from LAX with a couple of grand each in their pockets. Just a couple of guys going south for a good time, they would overnight in Ensenada, full of good little hotels, give OJ time to adjust to the temperature change.

Ensenada was on the coast, a major port, cruise ships, container movement and fair beaches with a population of around 280,000, a good place to get lost and have some fun, if you had that in mind. For them they would just lay up a couple of days and he would fill in OJ, then they would just drift on down to Pedro's, so for now they waited.

He contacted his contractor in Scotland and he needed two more days, then it was over for him. He picked up OJ at LAX Monday morning, with his old Ford pick-up and they drove to Ensenada, stopped in Tijuana and grabbed some tacos and a six-pack of Corona, and drove the 125k to Ensenada at a leisurely pace, enjoying the heat and the dry air that the Baja always gave. OJ never stopped talking unless he was eating or drinking, if there was a lull in the conversation he'd look across and sure as hell he was popping another top, or stuffing another taco in his face.

They laughed about old times and talked about the future. Maxine knew everything OJ did and if he did it, it was OK. They had both come from the wrong side of the tracks and moved to the other side, through hard work and hard drive, two clubs and both doing well, one was high-end the other was low-end, and both making money. When he got to thinking about it, he was the only one that didn't have another life, OJ had his clubs and wife and three kids, Pedro had his ranch and a great operation with a degree in agriculture, a hunting camp that brought a good 100,000 a year, a wife and three kids as well.

Chuck and Jim were the two singles, although Chuck had his surf shop and manufactured the top board in the US and was in the middle of negotiations for an outside company to produce them, he on the other hand, was buying into a ranch that needed help real bad. He knew nothing about ranching and helped brand a hundred head last fall and thought he still had the stink of burnt flesh in his clothes.

He felt like the old joke of the rancher who won the lotto, and his buddy said to him, 'what are you going to do now with all that money?' and he said 'I guess I'll just keep ranching till it is all gone.' God he hoped he was wrong!! But he enjoyed it just the same. And Mel and Linda were real special people. They didn't ask questions and he could come and go as he pleased. He couldn't ask for more than that. Fishing and all the hunting he could hope for, guess you had to start somewhere and ranching was more his type of work, once he got used to the winters. Although a rancher could make a living just selling hay and silage then close up for winter and go south, now that was more his type of ranching. He'd just have to wait and see.

CHAPTER 13

"LET'S TAKE A LOOK AT THE VEG," AND THEY ALL STUMBLED down the stairs to the basement, slipping on their masks as they went."

"Holy shit, you really have done a job on him, look at him drooling and just lying in it. What the fuck is that stink? Christ he's shit himself and pissed in it as well. OK, no question, he is brain dead and ready to go. I don't think he could find his arse with both hands, he is looking right at me and I'm sure he can't see a thing, and know what it is. You've done a great job lad, now wash him off before I gag, man he smells worse than your breath, well maybe not quite that bad, but almost. OK Stumps, no food or drink today, we take him back tonight, get to Oxford around 3am, drop him on a bench some place where he will be found, got it lad?"

"Aye aye Big Brother."

"Don't be taking the mickey Stumps, I'll give you a spanking."

"Fuck off John."

"Now now, the lad is really taking on an attitude these days."

"Aye, I think he has kind of taken to that lad, treating him like he was his own special little thing."

"Oh why don't you two fuckers leave me alone, I got things to do."

"OK Stumps, we leave after supper, just wrap him in a blanket, we'll dress him before we dump him, don't forget to throw some gloves in that van and maybe some arse wipe just in case you have to clean him up again."

"God forgive, but why did I have to be the youngest in this family?"

"Stumps, I just can't imagine the fucking mess we would be in if either of you two were the oldest."

"Christ, no wonder I drink! And I'm getting gray hair now, not surprising."

They were in the outskirts of Oxford by 2.30am.

"OK Stumps, get some clothes on him, and take care, gloves on first I don't even want a sweat gland to drip on this lad, from us, OK? Then take care with that nice white suit and get that tie just right, like he is going to another party, although he has had his last, I'd say."

"Hey John, should I put his shoes on the wrong feet, just for a joke?"

"See what I mean? This is not a fucking joke!

"NO! I'd better not see anything wrong when I dump him off, I want him just right, we get good money for this so no fucking jokes, got it? Now comb his hair and make it like the picture, rub in that gel shit then comb it fast, before it sets up."

"It doesn't set up Big Brother, it just sets it."

"Don't tell me you use that shit, only poofs use that stuff."

"Jesus John, everyone uses it, your kids use it. Where have you been? I'll bet you still use Brylcreem."

"Fucking right I do, that's for men though, don't worry yourself about that, you might be one someday, if I keep you right. Now just get the spick all looking pretty and we can get paid again."

"What do you think John, he looks good enough to fucking eat, ha ha!"

"Aye well don't you be getting all licky wi' him, what did I do to deserve this? Drop-off time is the first park bench we come to OK. Look, two benches outside the main gate, we will take the one on the south side, get that blanket out of the plastic bag, that's the one we carried him out in remember."

"Aye right, very appropriate I must say."

The van came to a smooth stop and the side door slid open and he was helped out and to the bench, then laid down, the blanket spread over him like a street person and over his head, and he didn't move. The van was gone, it was 3.30am and they were on their way home. The first truck stop on the M1 it pulled in between two long haul rigs and the plates were changed and magnetised decals removed, hubcaps replaced and back on the road.

"Hey John, are we going to stop again and eat?"

"Of course, I wouldn't let that tapeworm of yours go hungry now would I? Christ it must have been an hour since you had your last burger. I'll stop at the next nosh house and fill you up, Mickey 'Ds do you?"

"Could we try Wimpy's, I'm starting to dream about that fucking clown. What with all that money we are supposed to make I thought we might have a steak, or would that be stretching our budget? No fucking wonder Scotch folks get a bad name wi' lads like you bro."

"You know, my baby brother, I love you, with all your fucking faults, I love you, a steak it is, I could use one myself wi' a couple o' cackleberries on the side, how does that sound?"

"Just fine bro, just fine, maybe I should have two you know, to feed the worm and all," and they were both laughing.

CHAPTER 14

THEY HAD JUST GOT BACK FROM A MORNING SWIM, ordered breakfast and went up to change. His laptop was winking, he had mail. 'Third phase is now complete and the planting is done, the veggies are a great success. The best I've ever had. Good Luck. PS: I assume the check is in the mail. Yours forever, the Contractor.'

OJ was looking over his shoulder and shaking his head.

"That damned Scot never changes, does he?"

"I hope not," he said.

He gave him a look and nodded.

"Isn't that the truth? He never lets you down, him and his brothers, good warriors", and he looked back at the screen.

OJ said: "Remember after that raid we did two years ago in Angola and they were there, I got winged and couldn't do much? Well Maxine was having a bit of bother with the clientele, John showed up with the brothers and believe me the trouble went away, they damn near scared the good guys away as well. Then the addition to the old club, I got quotes from all over. Couldn't beat John's. I asked him, John you are not doing me any favors are you? And got the typical Scot answer, 'What tha fuck, you think I'm Santa or sumthin,' end of conversation.

"What amazes me is the clientele he has, if you are anyone in Glasgow and you haven't got some kind of structure from the Brothers 3 Construction Co. then you are not one of the in-group. What exactly did John do in the Rock Apes?"

"Gunner, sniper. That's where we met, on a course, they ran a small school at Bath Gate the home of 2-Para, he finished up there before demob."

"You are not supposed to get courses like that if you are a lefty or close to the door, like less than six months' service, but the Commander pushed it through. I thought he was doing me a favor but I think he had me on his home list, old bugger."

O J smiled.

"Well, what now?"

"Now we go to work. We will have breakfast, then head for the ranch. You haven't seen Chuck and Pedro for a while, have you?"

"No sir, but looking forward to it."

"Those two never change, not at all."

They slipped on shorts and T-shirts and headed down to eat. Jim paid the check and they threw their bags in the back and pulled out and south on Mex 1, to Maneadero. Pedro's ranch was off Mex 1 in the San Luis Mountains, close to the Mission San Luis Gunzaga. He had five hundred acres of everything, he grew blue agave and sold it to the tequila distilleries, and also for syrup, organic at that, it was so sweet they used it in their coffee, way better than sugar, then he had about a hundred head of the skinniest longhorn beef you have ever seen.

He asked Pedro once, 'What for? Why not Hereford, something with meat on it?' And he told him they don't eat them but sell them for the rodeo supply people, for roping and wrestling, they like them fast and lean. Then his hunting lodge was something special, 5000$ US a week, just great hunting. mountain lion, California Bighorn, wild pig, he told him he cheated and imported the pigs, the clientele never caught on and figured he had the biggest pigs in Mexico, not realizing they were well-fed. Pedro would take little dumps of hay and corn out to them.

Maria said it was her cooking that did it and it could have been, she sure could cook and always laid on a fine spread for them. And he knew the paying guests got the full treatment, fine wines and fine dining, and Pedro would walk around the table with a bottle of Tequila that was fifty years old and just pour, never asking, just pouring and that wasn't on the bill, and they loved it.

OJ talked till he fell asleep and Jim put the pedal down on their old pick-up, he wanted to make Guerrero Negro by night, then Pedro's by the next night, it was all go from then on. He had slipped a payment off to their Scottish contractors, thanking them for a fine job well done, hoping for bigger and better things in the future. John would take the boys out to Glasgow's finest, wives and kids and a little bonus check for all. It was good for the image of the company spending a little time with the rich folks and chatting about new structures and techniques and inviting new and past clientele to join them for cocktails. As rough around the edges as the three brothers were, they could sure turn on the charm. Their books were always full with pending jobs, 'Just how I like it lads,' and he would down another shot from the Isles.

CHAPTER 15

MEANWHILE IN BOSTON, A CODED MAIL FROM LONDON showed up, and the deciphering started. Globe and Mail page two. Short and sweet, she thought and started to bring up the Globe and Mail and scrolled to page two, the picture said it all. A young man reeling between two police officers with a blanket over his head, being escorted into an ambulance. Just below in bold print: 'Young man missing for five days returns from wild drug orgy in a state of complete disorder and unable to communicate with police, is escorted to an ambulance where he is taken to St Paul's for tests and observation. St Paul's stated he was being restrained at this time for his own good. Transportation from St Paul's to Panama was in the process of being arranged by his family.'

'Incidents like this were becoming far too frequent with the youth of today,' said a statement from the surgeon in charge. He said 'there was very little that could be done for this patient except proper care and patience and he went on to state that the drug problem with our youth was reaching the epidemic stage. And this must stop.'

'Well Barney that is news, how the hell did they

accomplish that? I'll likely never know and, don't want to know. But I'm not sorry for the arrogant bastard. I wonder how his family feel now.'

But indirectly she had been responsible for this, and didn't know just how to accept it, but would. She wanted the revenge just for herself and didn't want anyone else to know, it was her own private little war that those men were carrying out just for her.

CHAPTER 16

THE TOLL ROAD TO ENSENADA HAD BEEN RELATIVELY GOOD but any time you made on it was wasted with toll booths, but from there south, watch out, potholes you could hide a good pick-up in, then depending on the season the Vandoes would be full of water or a raging torrent. Vandoes were where they just paved right through the creek bed instead of a bridge. Hey they were talking economy here! This trip they were mostly dry, a little bit of whiplash to waken up your sleeping partner and they zipped on through, cops took cash and no receipts, saved time! More tacos and beer and they made Guerrero Negro by late afternoon.

They ate fresh fish and drank Corona and hit the sack early, first light found them on the road, they'd catch breakfast a couple of hours into the trip. A Mexican hotel wouldn't serve till 8 or 9, that would be uncivilized. They pulled off the pavement onto the gravel drive of Pedro's ranch, saying gravel, but that is only for the first fifty feet, the next twenty kilometers were just sand or dirt, you saw a rock on the road, you drove over it or around it, your choice depending on your wheels, he drove around.

They pulled into the ranch in a swirl of dust and

there were two dudes doing one armed push-ups for them, right out in the yard. Trying to show how good the ex-Seals were. OJ shouted:

"I could do that drinking beer, that's how they taught us in the UK Marines, so quit your shit and feed me, this nigger is starving, that damned Canuck wouldn't let me eat till we got here."

And there was a lot of back slapping and handshaking and 'how you doin's' going on. Cold beer was passed around and they sat on the porch, back in the shade and primed themselves up for things to come. They wouldn't talk job till later.

Maria came swishing out with a platter of snacks and there was more hugging and squeezing, then the kids came storming through and it all started all over again. OJ and Pedro were comparing kids.

"How you do that, I don't know", so Chuck and Jim just sat and listened, being the single guys. Not sure whether they were lucky or not. Jim kept saying he hadn't met the right one yet, and he felt that was true.

OJ said: "Shit man, you are 28 years old, better grab whoever will have you. And you Chuck coming from Texas, if you're not married by 17 you're ugly," and the laughter and banter went on into the night.

A guest cabin was set aside for them as the season wouldn't start for another month and the ranch was quiet and free of tourists and prying eyes. First light was always the most beautiful, the sunrise coming over the San Luis Mountains into Pedro's Valley always took his breath away and he was glad he could wake up to that every morning. He felt guilty taking him away from it to risk his life, when he had so much at stake. He came up and stood beside him and looked right at him, then shook his head.

"Don't even think about it, this is a choice I make and I wouldn't have it any other way.

"Come on, coffee is ready" and he pulled himself away from the rising sun that Mexico so took for granted. He got his brew and went and stood out on the porch with Pedro, they sipped and waited for the others to roll out.

"Ever miss the service Jim?"

He thought about it and shook his head.

"Not really, when I left it was time for me, I enjoyed it, I really did, some good friends. I didn't like all the bull and red tape, Yes Sir, No Sir, spent too much time with our hands tied when all you had to do was kick some ass, watched good people get hurt because of too many rules. You shoot at me! I'm going to blow your ass off and I won't stop till you are hamburger.

"Now that, the bad guys understand. Maybe it's wrong but I like what I do now. This guy killed this lady's daughter, oh he didn't mean to, but he did! And showed no remorse and for that he will pay an eye for an eye. I don't find that complicated. Now some folks would say it's not that simple. I say it is."

"I hear you man, that's the same thing, I couldn't swallow all this honor and dignity bull. I watched my comrades get cut down because they didn't have the order to defend themselves, do not show aggression and good men died because some senator, three thousand miles away didn't think it was that serious. I had to get out, and I came right down here to my home and if I leave again it will be for business only."

Chuck and OJ appeared still dripping from their morning showers.

"Is that coffee I smell OJ, we better get some before those two guzzle it all."

"Better do that, briefing at 0800 hours, the show starts today."

He spread his maps and aerial shots on the outside table held down with empty Corona bottles. Then he laid it all out. The only way the plan would change was if transport or weaponry didn't match the job, he'd ordered what they needed, now if they didn't get it, that could change everything.

Tomorrow they would leave, OJ and Jim in his pick-up, Chuck and Pedro in a ranch pick-up and head for Pichilingue just outside La Paz, catch the ferry to Mazatlan, 16 hours onboard if all went well. Then Mex 40 to Durango and at El Salto would be where they would catch their mystery flight to Panama, all being well. And the gear would be there, the Commander had never let him down in gear, it always came through. He wondered where he got it sometimes, but he never asked, it was always use and drop stuff so usually used before and picked up by the Commander and used for guys like them.

6am caught them making dust, pulling out of Pedro's ranch and heading south on Mex 1 and La Paz, they made it to the docks at El Salto with an hour to spare. The crossing was barely third class, barely! They slept on their luggage in the back of the pick-ups, that's why they still had luggage when they got there. Pedro made the point that they were poor folks, and gringos were fair game. So always someone was on the back of the boxes. They went ashore and headed for Mex 40 and the road to Durango; at 75k the sign pointing into the mountains said El Salto, he thought it was a joke.

Pedro took offence and said you probably didn't like my driveway either, what could he say, the other two were snickering behind his back. It amazed him that El Salto could be as big as it was with a road like that, and there on the outskirts was the strip, two hangars and five planes from an ultralight to the twin-prop Dakota. One looked like a duster and the other two looked in excellent condition and fast and that spoke for it. Cartel, likely from Guatemala or Nicaragua just taking on some fuel. El Salto had maybe fifty houses, a bar that sold auto parts and pumped gas right from the truck. You could get something to eat there as well, but they weren't taking the chance, the last thing they needed was some guys with the runs and the leg shakes.

Jim drove right to the most prominent looking hangar and was met by a guy with a black cowboy hat, a ponytail and an M16, and not smiling. He asked for Romano and he gestured with the M16 to the other hangar. He gave him his gracies and left immediately, don't piss a guy off with a gun, especially if you don't have one. Now on the second look this didn't look too good, pretty beat up, some tin missing and the blanks filled in with plywood. He tapped on the side door.

He didn't want to hit it too hard in case he caused structural damage. The pilot could hear them coming from inside and the door swung open. The guy that opened it was as blond as Chuck, about 5' 8" well-built and a big smile.

"Hey! You guys must be my passengers, great, been waiting for you", he didn't say how long.

"Park your rigs and come on inside, your stuff is OK here. Oh, I'm Cable." So Jim introduced the guys and himself, all just first names and wrong ones at that, but likely as real as Cable, they would maybe never see this guy again after this little foray, but who knew.

Right off to one side was a beautiful little Lear jet, it had Cartel written all over it, he made the comment,

"Fancy wings," and Cable looked at him and smiled.

"Yeah, that's your ride, you boys get to travel in style this trip" and Jim was aghast.

"How the hell did the Commander arrange that, it looked about an eight seater."

"I can make it to your drop zone and back to Nicaragua before refuelling, then back here, and catch a ride back to Nicaragua and I'll be your jockey for the extraction. Got a nice little Blackhawk for that. You'll love it, even got gun mounts, this sucker was built for Desert Storm and never went, just one of those things, so it's in mint condition. So don't worry, your travel arrangements are all first class, oh that crate in the corner is yours, right?"

"Great, I want to see how close the old boy came to my order," the crate was about 8' by 4' and 3' high, he looked around for a wrecking bar and Cable handed him one.

"I'm going to nip in to the village and grab something to eat, that will give you time to sort it all out. OK, gas up your trucks and bring them inside and park them in the corner, just leave me enough room to get this baby out, leave the doors open and we will roll within the hour, OK?"

"Thanks Cable, that should do it." Pedro and OJ went to take care of the trucks, Chuck and Jim headed for the crate. Chuck smiled at him and said:

"My curiosity is killing me."

"Just wait and see," he said and laughed, and he gave him a funny look.

He started prying the strapping off the crate, finally freeing the lid they both lifted it off and stacked it against the hangar wall. First thing out was a layer of bubble wrap, then four black 'chutes for the night drop. Chuck reached in and pulled out a stack of flak jackets, all strapped together and screws up his face giving him a funny look, "What the hell are these for, I thought you didn't care for this type of stuff."

"Take a look at them," he said and he cut the strapping with a pocket knife and they all popped open. He slowly removed one and held it up in the poor light and started to smile.

"Now this is definitely one of your ideas," and he started to laugh.

"Maybe one of your better ones." The vests were black and emblazoned on the left top was a name in Spanish blanked out, on the right and the back was the crest of the Panamanian Drug Enforcement Squad and it stated so in large letters. Black shirt, combat pants and boots.

"Shit man, we could go to jail for impersonating these guys."

He laughed and replied:

"Shit man, we could go to jail anyway for what we are about to do. Then he said:

"They don't have many blond dicks down here."

He reached in and pulled out slipover balaclavas of fine cotton, eyes and mouth-holes and perforated around the nose for better breathing. The quality was DEA, without a doubt that is where they came from.

"The CIA and DEA went to Panama and trained a whole pile of Panamanian Federalists to be drug busters and they got very good at it.

"Then they found out they could get a little better money fighting in Afghanistan for the Mercs, like from $9 a day to 300US, the choice was simple. Next out of the box were Kevlar Logistical Helmets, Chuck was looking at them real close and turning them around, then he slipped one on and felt the keypad on the side and dropped the visor and saw the readout screen, with drop-down night vision.

"Where the hell did he get these from? I gotta know."

He just shook his head.

"No way, I never ask and the surprises keep coming, that is good enough for me."

"Yeah, you're right, no point in complicating a good thing."

"The thing is, if the Commander wasn't in the business, I don't think I could work for anyone else, I don't want to be involved in any of those big ops, company strength or even close. I like what I have."

And Chuck nodded. "Me too, I've never thought about it, but I like this group, it's kind of personal like family and I always feel like I'm doing the right thing, even though it is wrong by the law, that is."

"Well that is how I feel, in the last couple of years I've kind of worked myself into a position where I could scrape by if I never did it again, financially that is, but now I've got myself involved with this ranch, I don't know, I've spent a lot of money lately, the nest egg just got eaten." He looked at Chuck and he was smiling and shaking his head.

"I'd never thought about it, but sometimes I sit and think what does Jim do, besides fish, we all know about the fiber optics and the leather sales and I could see you fixing communication stuff but never dealing with the public, no way, I just don't see you putting up with some of the shit I have to live through, some people are so fucking stupid it scares me!

"But a ranch, dude, that is a way off track for me, shit that makes you a cowboy or a farmer, I just don't believe it, hey but if that's what turns you on, you do it man, just do it, it's what has to be right for you. So I guess you are going to go home and buy a tractor?"

"Did that the last time, now it is going to be a baler, one of those round type 600 pounders, that's big enough."

"Wow man, you've even got the size all figured out. Wait till I tell Pedro, he is going to chew your ear off, it won't be nice." He reached into the box and pulled another layer of bubble wrap off, 'ho ho ho, what have we got here then?' and he pulled up four shoulder rigs, each one had a slot for a suppressor with one in it and believe it, one is left-handed, that old boy is something special. The hand guns are Makarov 9mm semi-auto with an eight-round clip and three extra clips for each pistol, good. Chuck was handling one, pulled it down and looked over the parts, he slowly nodded:

"Not bad, used but not abused."

"Load one up and stick on the suppressor, then throw a couple of shots into the corner of the hangar fast, I want to see if they are as good as they look, these are Russian, they were good, supposed to be, same thing was made in Bulgaria and aren't worth a shit."

Chuck grabbed a box of ammo and wandered over to the corner and started pumping shells in.

"I think they hold eight, good enough."

Under that, laid end-to-end were three Dragunov 7.62 sniper rifles, very nice. He picked one up and looked into the dark side of the hangar with it, good, real good, lots of light pick up, all they needed, they would maybe get three or four rounds out of each and then abandon, seemed a shame but they didn't want the extra weight, and a long barrel like that would likely get hung up going through a door and maybe get you shot, so they pulled the bolts, and dropped them. Maybe pick them up later, maybe! Right beside them was this ugly looking thing, looked like a kid's plastic toy, all yellow and green, he pulled it out. Chuck looked back and scowled,

"What the fuck is that?"

"That, my good man is mine, it's called an FPS but really an AA12 fully auto 12 gauge shotgun, holds 20 rounds in a drum mag, recoil is nil, can fire that and drink tea and it will open any door that we will come to, and an excellent street sweeper, can empty a hallway in seconds."

"Wow, are we going to have fun or what? I can feel the blood rising already," and he turned and aimed the pistol into the top corner and squeezed the trigger rapidly and emptied it out, and turned to Jim and nodded.

"Feels good and works good, I like it."

"Take a look at this", and he threw one to him,

"It's an AK 104 7.62mm assault rifle, mag hold 30 and gets rid of them at 600rpm, good gun, not for house clearing but you can't win them all, I asked for something short and 9 mm, but this will do the job, same ammo as the sniper pieces anyway. We got four of them, now come the goodies."

OJ and Pedro were backing the pickups into the corner, side by side in case they wanted to get out fast, who knew.

Jim waited and waved them over,

"Come and see the toys, plenty for everyone," and he started laying them out.

"There are twelve Light Armor RPG 18s, thirteen pounds each, ready to kill, 27 inches long, a little awkward to carry but we will use them up fast and get rid of them, a little overkill, they can penetrate 1 inch of armor, I don't think we will find that but they will do the job and sure as hell cause confusion. Three twelve-packs of hand grenades, HE, smoke and flash bangs.

"All great for surprise stuff, it causes real confusion. If you really use them up it gets the weight down as we are going to be really packing on the go, so the quicker we unload, the better."

There were a couple of medium cardboard boxes still unopened and Pedro pointed to them.

"What's with those?"

Jim just nodded,

"The icing on the cake, but I'll explain later, let's get all this stuff on board so we can get out of here when that Cable guy gets back. Hey that's quick, the Cable Guy."

So they started loading in great haste, Jim saw OJ looking at a small bale of 12 pairs of combat gloves, some with no fingers, those are great things for climbing or loading, the finger ones for the rough work.

"That old fart didn't miss much, did he?" he said. "I hope not, because what he misses we'll miss more, and that's a fact. There are only four of us and if they knew that, we wouldn't stand a chance, even if we were the real drug squad, four they would take out sooner or later. So our mission will be to create an illusion of numbers. That being done by surprise, confusion, noise and destruction."

And he now felt they had the means, after opening the Commander's goody box he felt a lot more confident, in fact he felt good. They were just loading the last box and sliding the crate into the corner when Cable came wheeling in to the hangar driving an old GMC Tracker, all beat to ratshit, no doors, no top, but running with a Mex passenger beside him.

He gave Jim a nod, the hangar manager closed doors, opened doors and said nothing, his kind of guy.

"Hey great, all loaded" and he climbed up the ramp and handed Jim a large Thermos.

"Coffee is hot and sweet, so let's fly."

He hit a button on the side and the ramp lifted up and in. Two nice little Rolls-Royce turbos, started their wind-up and it took about ten and they started to leave the hangar. He made straight for the closest end of the runway, did a quick spin around and faced right into their own dust, counted to about ten and they lurched ahead. OJ was on his hands and knees everyone was scrambling for seats and belts and laughing. The com came on and Cable said:

"Sorry guys, no ladies this trip you, will have to figure out the seats yourself. I'm going to stay low till out of Mexico then lower, but I will get you up for your drop" and they could hear him laughing.

"Hey Jim, come up front and we can discuss this thing."

So he climbed up the deck that felt about 45% at this time and joined him in the co-pilot's seat.

"Just wait till we get kind of leveled off and hear if anyone is asking for me, if no-one is asking, no-one knows, just what we want."

It took about fifteen and he said:

"OK, fill me in, I've got the route and the destination. What I want is time of drop that will give me my speed and any changes, God forbid."

"The only change is location," and he looked at him fast, with a worried look,

"What? Don't piss me off, please don't."

"Not a problem, I didn't say anything to the guys but there were no tanks for a high altitude drop, so what you do is take us to about ten thousand, and one ridge before the drop zone drop us at the extraction point, that will make it about three miles shorter for you and longer for us. I don't like to use the same location twice but in this case it will work as we will be coming out the same way we go in from the back door."

"Oh that's no big deal, you scared me, I thought you might want more mileage out of this, and there is no more to give, when I come down in Costa Rica it will be on fumes, so whatever you give me will be good."

"How big is the extraction landing?"

"Maybe an acre or more like two, close."

"Great that's a good DZ, real good."

"Now, as this is our extraction as well, be aware for bad guys."

"You can't be the only one that knows about this spot, don't even think about it."

"I know that, but there isn't a village or a trail within seventy miles of thick jungle."

"That is where you could run into trouble as there is only the one trail out the back and that is it, so if they don't know you went that way, all the better, but if they do, all they have to do is follow you, as there is nowhere else to go. Now if there is a chopper there take it out because that could put them there before you, you have a good twenty miles to go to get there, they could be sitting waiting for you with some guys bringing up the rear, you got no way out! I'll do what I can but that won't be much."

They flew on in silence for a while as Jim sat and sorted it out. If the intell was good there should be no problems, but who knew, and he let it run around in his head again, and again. The guys were catching some zee time and he should too, but that wouldn't work till he was completely satisfied. He didn't sleep with problems, solve them, then sleep like a baby. If you can do something about it, do it. If not, don't worry about it, but be ready to live with it.

Cable got to talking about his flying time in Afghanistan desert raids and jungle runs for his bosses he worked for today, there was no question he hauled for the Cartel, maybe their target was a customer, this didn't come up. But he could tell he wasn't altogether happy with his lot. This chopper that was picking us up he was paying for it, hardly making any money. But trying to get a name out there for him was a tough job.

"This chopper that I'm picking you up with is a Blackhawk, just the best, flies like a bullet, got all the bells and whistles. I don't know how long I'm going to have it available, it's up for sale."

"How much?" he asked.

"One point five big ones."

"Just a little rich for my budget."

"I tried to buy it on time, like by the job but, no way, he wanted cash. Wants a bigger one to haul his buds to his island, would you believe?

"And this is one of my good customers, all legit guys, not like the other shit I work for, but where the hell do you get real bucks today without bending the rules a little?"

"What would you do with that chopper if you had it, how would you make it pay?"

"Easy, got all kinds of good legitimate work."

"But you must have your own rig."

"Well no point in dreaming, the good fairy can't seem to find me, I tried the bank, even tried the bad boys, no buddy wants to deal me in, high risk I suppose, so that is that and it won't last.

"It is a great rig, got some hidden extras that would scare the shit out of you," and he gave him that sly look and a wink, like he was supposed to know.

Jim crawled through the back and picked a lounger and tried to catch some shut-eye, once they hit the deck it would be on limited quantities, with no quality. He got a three hour shake before doors opened.

When that call came through the earpiece, he thought he must have forgotten something, it felt like he'd just placed his head on the rest, when the call came. He walked around kicking feet and pouring coffee.

"OK merry men, let's gear up," and they started strapping on tools and all that was needed, they had so much gear they would run static lines with containers, this would hang fifteen feet below you off one thigh, it put a little list to you but gave you a little warning before you hit ground, unless you ended up in a tree, not fun.

Once all geared up and containers loaded with each of their special equipment for the chores he designated, they gathered around the table and he filled everyone in to the last detail.

All joking aside now this was what they got paid for. Chuck was Jim's liaison and things funneled through him. He talked to Cable through his com and got a twenty minute to drop time, he would climb in ten thousand, then once they were out he would drop fast and turn and be gone. At ten thousand feet they could jump and open in five, giving them ninety-five to the drop zone. You opened high and no-one would hear the crack of the 'chute, if you're close to the ground someone could hear that crack or maybe two or three, and away up in high country like that, there was no-one just dropping in for a cup of tea. So they wouldn't be long in figuring out that they were up to no good. In that neck of the woods they were the bad guys, so they sat and waited. Those minutes before an active drop were long ones. With five to go, they all stood and faced the door and checked their gear and they checked the guy in front, as he couldn't see his back, but you could. Then they all turned around and did the same again, then started to shuffle to the door, holding on to the containers, the static line was folded back and forward on your pants and would rip free after you were airborne, but they were going to drop five first, their chances of being spotted were remote but you took your chances and hoped for the best, no verbal contact till ground contact, and right then the seal broke on the door and you could hear the rush of air. They pulled their goggles on and waited till the door folded up and in, no lights. Cable came on and said "hold." The lights had gone out when the door opened and he tipped his wing and said "Go"! Jim was gone, OJ was touching him and Pedro was touching him, Chuck was herding and stepping on Pedro's heels.

Five seconds and they were all airborne, Jim looked over his shoulder, he could just see the little plane drop and turn and disappear into the dark. He glanced at his GPS strapped on his wrist and veered to the right at ninety-five hundred, he opened and felt the snap of the rigging and the container slide off the bottom and swung off his left leg. Shit, it was dark, the moon was just a sliver, without night vision it wouldn't have been pretty trying to avoid the trees. He felt his body come straight, the container was down and so was he. He dropped and rolled and tore off his harness, his Makarov 9mm was in his hand and he waited and heard the others hit down, the little grunts you make when you compress and roll. Tommy 'chutes were three feet smaller in diameter than the US 'chutes thus you came down a lot faster, less time in the air, less time of being spotted or shot. Some guys hadn't read the Geneva Convention and some didn't give a shit. They headed for the treeline and blended in and waited, he gave it ten and broke silence and got a count, all down in good shape. Success. He moved out using the GPS and it took him to a small entrance, to a trail, it was still quite dark, not much moon, a little cloud, meager stars. They had about five hundred meters to go to a small clearing and they would lay up till light, get orientated, organized and move out.

The clearing was the size of a small back yard and they slunk back into the brush and unloaded, they were all packing a good load. Chuck, OJ and Jim had Dragunov 7.62 sniper rifles with eight rounds of Mach grade ammo to carry, besides the AK104s with five 30-round mags and besides that, Jim was carrying the shotgun with five 20-round mags, a little overkill but could be useful, they each had three RPG Light Armor shoulder grenades, could penetrate one inch armor, they were 27 inches long and loaded weighed 13lbs each. Pedro had his little surprise to place, it weighed close to 10lbs, then an assortment of HE, smoke and flash bangs, the HE was to kill you with, the smoke was for them to get lost in and the flash bangs in a closed room would temporarily blind you and the bang was so severe it could make you bleed from the ears, and totally disorientate them long enough for them to do what they wanted. Live or die. So the guys were carrying about 95lbs, Jim with his shotgun had 100, that included a meager ration of food, with three water bottles. The hardest thing with all that weight was to remain silent and maneuverable, after the first shot was fired the weight would start to fall off. But until then it was suffer, baby, suffer. They took an hour about, so they got three hours sleep at a run, that was good, they had set out listening devices at a hundred yards in three locations, all facing downhill towards the target, as that was the source of the trail and they were at the end or just about.

First light came at close to 05.00 hours, just a few filtering streaks in the sky where they could see it, the canopy above them was close to 150 feet or more, of fine timber, Panama produced a large collection of timber, sold all over the world, teak, mahogany, Spanish cedar and spiny cedar which had long spikes on it, but a beautiful wood. Almendro, rosewood, balsamo, and Amarillo, all being logged faster than it could be re-planted, but it left a fairly open forest and it made it easier to travel in. The noise was horrendous with all the birds screaming their welcome or bugger off calls. Pedro was their point man on a continuous basis, which seemed a little unfair.

Pedro looked and acted like a Ghurkha, in the woods he was part of, and blended in, to perfection and could move so fast through the timber it was like gliding.

They all thought they were pretty good in the bush and they weren't bad, but compared to Pedro they were an elephant stampede, that is how Pedro described them anyway.

Little remarks like "how you guys have lived this long in the bush I don't know, I could hear you coming a mile away, which one of you guys is carrying the bell, it's keeping me awake."

So fuck him, he had a point, when you are that good that is where you should be, they would do three miles and re-group and take a little rest, no hurry, he wanted to get there in time to stake the place out before dark, set up hides, and do a four-point reckon. Each of them taking a designated area, and the next day the same again, but they would rotate the locations, that way you could maybe pick up on something the other guy missed, had to check times of guard changes, how many, and the big one, outside surveillance, they didn't want them watching when they thought they were watching them. It was out there, no question HDS cams in trees, trip wires, lasers, ground mikes, just little things on spikes like a nail and you stuck it into the ground and it did its job very well, you could only find them with a scanner and you'd better be good because they were.

They had all their Panamanian DEA gear packed in their packs, those flak jackets would have dissolved them in the humidity, they would don the fancy gear before the raid. So they moved on down the trail, it was no more than a game trail, it got steep at times and Jim wondered about the return trip, uphill all the way, but they would be traveling light, he thought. Approximately half way down the trail they set up an HDSC, that way they could check their trail and see if anyone had traveled it since them, just so they would know if it was well used or not, the way it looked it hadn't been used in a while, but who knew? They weren't taking any chances, not now, not ever, he liked to take everyone home in one piece, he'd never used a body bag for any of his guys yet, and hoped he never would.

# CHAPTER 17

WHEN HE FIRST CAUGHT SIGHT OF IT, IT LOOKED LIKE ONE of those Swiss castles built on the mountainside, all cream concrete and red tile roofs with a turret at each end, large rounded doors facing the front and a parking spot for a couple of vehicles, it was a magnificent home. Three levels with a tiled roof and dormers all along the front and little shutters on all the frames. The second level had a number of large deck areas, one in the centre with a rounded balustrade facing out over the parking area and the front door, it looked twenty feet deep and a good forty long and this is where there was a large dining room table, very elaborate, heavily carved legs rounded at each end, maybe twelve or fourteen feet long. Against the back wall of the house were serving tables with warming trays and all kind of paraphernalia for the staff, with two of them at it right now in nice light grey dresses and white aprons with bibs and little pin-on hats you expected to see housemaids wearing at the Embassy Ball. These guys liked to live in style, two sets of French doors opened onto this large deck, with a scattering of occasional chairs in the corners, with small tables so someone could have a cocktail before dinner and just lounge around, or walk to the balcony and watch the peons working on the garden below, then below that was where the real peons were at work, making the bucks that allowed all this to go on, quite a set up.

Everything seemed very relaxed and pristine, they found a hide and dropped their gear, then fanned out to their fields of fire, and observed. Jim brought the binos into play and did some serious snooping, trying to cover every inch of ground inside and outside the compound, without moving. He figured the whole area was ringed with a chainlink eight feet or more high, with a ring of razor wire on top, but in very bad shape, he was quite surprised. Other Cartel locations they had hit in the past for different reasons were always very high tech, latest in weaponry and surveillance technology.

There was another balcony that hung over the gorge below, it was a little smaller and seemed mainly for surveillance, with no-one on it. Noise wasn't a problem, the birds kept up a steady squawk and chatter, it was so bad someone could walk right up on you, so it was swivel neck time for sure.

There are 972 different species of birds in Panama and he thought they were all having a convention right now, in their location!! Right below that patio was the front door, it had to be eight feet high by six wide, two parking slots and a driveway cut into the stone, heading straight down to the valley floor. They were looking right down on the tops of two concrete block buildings, in line, approximately twenty feet wide by forty feet long, right where they should be, according to the print.

Then after that, about another twenty feet apart,

were the three iron sheds where the work took place, the sorting and the drying, only trouble there now were four. Shit, now they were a rocket short. The whole gorge was covered with a net suspended from side to side, and the whole length at least four hundred feet long, the gorge was no more than a hundred feet wide. From their vantage point they could see right through it, but from the air it would look like a dark gorge, the airstrip had to be four hundred yards to their south-west on the other side of the gorge, so the road had to cross under the net to climb up to it, at least, and sure as shit, a chopper sat right beside two small single prop jobs.

He couldn't tell, but it seemed a fair size behind the small aircraft. He just wondered if they could throw an RPG that far and score a hit, that would be Chuck's job. The table on the patio was being set for the evening meal, he assumed, and hoped this might give them a clue as to where everyone sat, another necessary point. All three snipers had to have a clear shot.

So they waited, Jim had his notepad out, lying beside him, making little sketches on it and notes and he knew the others were doing the same. He had seen three guards all carrying M16s and they looked old, that could mean malfunction, the M16 was the main piece in the US army in Vietnam so they could be 50 years old, he was surprised, he had expected to be out-gunned, but the AK104s were a decade ahead of the M16s. These guards wore white shirts and nice slacks, it seemed they were more interested in what went on inside rather than outside, they looked fat and overfed, nice cowboy boots all shined up, not something you would like to chase a bad guy in.

He could tell they were more concerned with internal security rather than external, definitely been at it too long without any outside threats, all that was going to change, real soon. Oh yeah!! They set up HDSC, each of them had two and they picked their spots, then crawled back out of sight and made a little hide. He set up the PC and brought in their cams, all seemed to be working, but some needed adjusting, that they would take care of first, once they got good observation positions they could check their locations before going to them, keep count of guards and their routines.

There were only four of them, so they couldn't keep watch on everything, so the cams helped a lot. They would just abandon them when the op was finished, they would probably hang on a tree till the tie strap rotted off or the tree fell down. They were no more than two inches square and an eighth of an inch thick, with a battery no bigger than you would put in your Timex, if anything passed in front they would snap it and your PC would give you the wink. They tried one at 100 yards and had it zoom that table in till you could see what they were eating, it was beyond him, the quality of this equipment the old Commander had put together for them, so they watched.

Dinner was a long affair, a lot of discussion going on. Now get this, at the head of the table sat Mum, to her left sat Dad and beside him sat Junior, with a servant or nanny and she was spoon feeding him.

Then led away the same way he arrived, it seemed he

couldn't make it on his own or speak, as no-one spoke to him but the nanny, and she continually dabbed his chin or wiped his face. He guessed the saying should be don't piss off the Scots or they will fuck you up real good. That boy was history, never to recover, Jim could see that.

He selected three sniper hides for their principal kills, with secondary shots taken from the same location. All hides had good back door routes to their next locations and targets at that point Chuck would take out the front door with his first RPG, OJ and Jim would take the two concrete block buildings, they had small windows high up in the walls at the rear, facing them, no glass, just mesh vents high up in the gable end.

Both RPGs would go through them, not even a hard shot, if they missed the mesh it didn't matter as long as they hit the back wall of the building, then their next two would take the first and second tin sheds, Chuck would throw two smokes and a flash bang. He had an arm like a baseball player, then he could take shed 3 with an RPG and Jim would take shed 4. He would have one left and Chuck as well, his next target would be the chopper, if it was possible, but he would have to try.

Jim's last RPG would go to a 2000lbs propane tank placed one hundred feet parallel from the house, with a small walking path to it, and above all the other structures that would cause a ball of fire that you would see in Panama City, and more confusion than Mardi Gras, and would probably take out a good piece of the cliff and send it down on the buildings below or what was left of them.

This was going to work, he could feel it. It was going

to take place at the noon meal, it seemed to be their principal meal and that would give them time to make it back to their DZ or point of entry, now their extraction point, their one weak factor.

Normally he would never use the point of entry as their point of exit, you just didn't do it. There are at least two good books of intense writing describing why you don't extract on entry points and he wasn't going in to it. It was wrong, but they were going to do it as the choices were nil. But he didn't have to like it, he would feel better if Chuck made a strike on that chopper, a lot better. He checked his watch and it was time to get back to their principal hide and discuss what everyone had found out, then go back for two-night op locations.

They would move twice during the night and just watch and take a few notes, what really surprised him was no outside patrols. The fence was chainlink and in poor shape, leaning in and fractured in a couple of places, where maybe a vehicle had bumped it and stretched it and it bulged out like a catch-net. He had also seen where animals had dug under the wire and made entry looking for food, so it didn't look like there was an alarm system in place, of course this could all be a bluff and they might just let it look like that, but he had his doubts.

Chuck and OJ were back and snacking up, that was all they had, oatmeal blocks, cookies, corned beef hash, nuts and raisins, in small Ziploc bags, as they didn't make a noise when opened. They took a lot of precautions, they even had light skins for their boot soles that hooked on the front and you pulled up the back, this would hide all the tread and leave no real tracks, just smudges which they kept to a minimum. He was beginning to think all these precautions were a waste, but better safe than sorry, one screw up and they could all be dead. He had just watched the evening meal on the large patio and it was identical to the night before, the two guards in the background were different, the maids serving were the same, the nanny was the same. He hadn't seen a guard that wasn't 40 or plus, this was all good. They had all their locations secure, all they had to do now was occupy them before first light, prime their RPGs and grenades and wait till noon. The signal for the operation to commence would be Jim's laser dot, he would place his crosshair on the target's heart and when ready, press the laser light and the dot would appear on his chest that was the signal to fire, then they would break radio silence, but not until. Just in case.

He was astounded at the lack of security and wondered if they had sound sensors that would pick up radio signals, maybe he was grasping at straws, but something was formulating in his mind and it was that they had never been hit before and that maybe they were being left alone on purpose, good kickbacks could take care of a lot. And they knew he had friends in high places, very high! It just made him nervous and it was close now, by this time tomorrow they would be on their way out in the chopper, sounded good and he fell asleep. He got his nudge at midnight, just as his watch started to vibrate on his wrist and he slipped out to his prearranged post.

The moon was three-quarter, with a little cloud, not much, the insects were making their music and he slid in to get eaten alive, but a good spot, the only lights were the front door and four yard lights. Down below, the living quarters for the workers was off to the rear and behind a chainlink fence, this was good as they wouldn't lose anything in the disaster, as that was where they were going to cause a disaster, he hoped! He lay there in his hide and went over the plan again, it had all been agreeable to the others but he still worried, in case he'd missed anything and they'd had their input and always constructive. He started to let his mind wander and was thinking about hay and balers, he almost laughed out loud and was having a little shake to himself. So to get back on track, he took the spotter and went over all the locations to watch for. He could see smoke rise from a corner of the house and a white shirt was taking a leak outside and having a smoke at the same time, just wide open, he thought he could have walked up to him and asked for a light, and he would have given him one. Shit, too easy, just too easy, and he worried some more.

He crawled back to the hide and started to slip on his Panamanian outfit, high top boots, pulled off the skins and buried them, right where he sat, with his Gerber he cut them into pieces and stuck them into a little hole and packed it down good. He was fumbling with the flak jacket when Pedro showed up and started the same maneuver, they got all geared up and had something to eat, leaving very little and one bottle of water from now till out. They were going to need it on the climb-out, that was for sure.

OJ was next, then Chuck and they all got it done and removed the name tags from the shirts, that would be a no-no, went over the plans again and disappeared back to their principal locations, this was their location hide for their first kill shots, then once the RPGs had done their work it was open season, he hoped!

He nestled down in his hide, had a pee and a dump before leaving the other guys, and buried it, and they had their turn and followed suit, eating those rations could cut down on your movements, which wasn't bad, if a guard had walked past he could smell that or a dog definitely and that could blow the whole thing so they kept it away from their hides and well back, without a walk in the woods that is, sometimes on a snipe you would have to shit in your hide or maybe in your pants if they were right on top of you, then dogs could be a big threat, a lot of those people didn't realize how valuable dogs could be, all they saw was something they had to feed or walk around the perimeter, then cage up and clean up after them.

Foolish thoughts, some dogs were worth two guards, especially like the team they'd been watching, they seemed more worried about their white shirts and their creases in their pants and he was sure he'd got a whiff of cologne in the evening breeze the night before, it wasn't his, they'd taken sweat gland pills, they neutralize any odor your body tends to dispense, their clothes had been sprayed with a neutraliser to remove any odor, the same type of thing a bow hunter would use. If you have to let that animal get close you'd better not be dispensing any foreign odor to him, or you are going to be a hungry hunter, and the same applied to them, Gurkhas say they could smell sweaty feet inside army boots.

Now before settling in for the night Jim went to his

secondary hide. This was where he would fire his RPGs from, all three, it was totally hidden from the house and below he could just see the roofs of his targets, so that meant no-one could see him. He set up his three RPGs, primed them, opened the sights, took a practice aim, then placed them on the ground at the base of a small mahogany tree, evenly spaced and covered them with grass and leaves. All he had to do was pull the pin, aim and fire, some didn't have pins, these Ruskies did, just a safety feature. The old Commander must have had a secret buddy in the Kremlin as every piece of artillery we had was from the Soviet Republic, all good stuff, but made him wonder. So after that little bit of prep, he went to his entry point that he had chosen for himself and crawled to the wire, and removing his small hand-held laser cutter, he slowly zapped each strand of the chain link and cut himself an entry hole, leaving it in position by the merest thread in four places, so all he had to do was hit it running and it would fold in front of him, this cutter was totally silent and just left a slight odor of cut metal and only for a very short time. Wire cutters would snap and in a quiet dawn could be heard a long way away. He went back to his principal hide and snuggled in, set his watch and closed his eyes and tried to snooze till first light.

He felt the first pulse on the back of his wrist and was a little surprized that he had slept. He lay and listened for any foreign sound, or no sound, he slid his spotter up on its short tripod with its little tube covering the lens, this would cut reflection, not 100% maybe 85, but that remaining 15 was what could kill you, all it took was one glimmer and it could cause a question and someone would come for an answer, game over.

He swept the compound below and saw heads washing and lining up at a bench, which must have been a cooking facility, not quite the standards of the folks in the big house. Within the hour they were shuffling into the large tin buildings. From the back of the big house half a dozen older lads in white coats emerged from a side door in the big house, some were smoking, as they headed for the block buildings where they met four other men from the poorer end of the compound, and they stood around the doors to the building smoking and chatting, they seemed to be waiting for something.

One of the white shirts appeared from the same door wiping his hands and wearing a Stetson of light gray, very classy, this shirt thought he was something, he wore a gun belt with a tied down holster and a white handled pistol in it, real Western style, right to the boots, one hand leaning on the grip he strolled over to the group and started chatting and laughing out loud at some joke one of them had made, he pulled a key ring off his belt and proceeded to open the door of the first building and waved them in, three white coats and two workers went in and he closed the door and locked it again, then with the other three went to the next building and did the same thing.

He got the feeling he was not locking in, but rather locking out, it didn't matter they were toast at noon. After completing that little chore he lit a smoke and looked around and up to their area, Jim felt he was looking right at him again, and he was, but he just didn't know it. He knew he couldn't see him, he always got a rush when that happened. He then turned and strolled back to the side door and went in, show over, till breakfast for the royalty, that was another two hours.

Then it was maids setting tables and two guards leaning over a balustrade looking down at the top of the net, smoking then taking position in their designated spot against the wall, and the family entered, fruit juice was poured and Jim could almost smell the bacon, sons-of-bitches. He swore he was going to eat a pound of that nice crispy stuff when this little foray was over. Everything practically the same as the day before, now he just prayed for the same at lunchtime, then they could get this show on the road.

His hide was about 100 feet from the fence and raised so he was looking onto the balcony, just enough to get the job done and he was sorting all this out in his mind when he happened to glance down and there was a little column of what looked like racoons, ma and three babies, one riding on her back, two tagging along, they were heading for the fence and a little scratch-hole that would take them under. Well that old girl started under that fence and junior on her back was squealing like crazy, well the whole breakfast team were all at the railing watching the antics, the nanny even had young Martinez up to see the game, so he took a quick scan over the group, the kid was toast, just looking but seeing nothing, Dad was a debonair looking kind of guy, nice gray hair, all wavy and fairly long, very classy, neatly combed little moustache, well-trimmed, could have been any of our fathers, very pleasant smile and making some kind of joke with the guard.

Now ma was a different package, been a real looker in her day, the high cheek bones and black hair pulled back and up into some kind of pile on her head, with a silver comb stuck in it, looked the real Spanish lady, but those lips, not a smile crossed them, more like a sneer. She said something and the banter stopped and every one returned to the table and resumed their breakfast.

What froze him in place was the fence, that damned racoon was all hung up about six feet from where he had cut his entry hole. He thought it would fall in, and that they couldn't miss seeing it, as it was five high and three wide, but then baby fell off and ma waddled through and the two wee ones followed, and right at that time was when the Martinezes were ordered back to the table to resume breakfast. Close call, way too close for his liking, he didn't realize that he'd been holding his breath, he lowered his face into the grass and slowly exhaled, feeling the sweat trickling down his spine and under his arms and he deep breathed for a while, it was going to be a long morning that damned Kevlar hat was making his head itch, he never did care for head protection.

So they waited, the table was cleared and everyone left, except one of the guards who was having his smoke, hanging over the balcony, same position as before, his forearms resting on the balustrade. He was staring right at Jim so he closed his eyes and just lay there and counted, a minute later when he opened them, he had turned away and now had his back to him, he turned and threw his butt to the parking lot below and left.

It was quiet time again and he just lay and wiggled his toes inside his boots and watched below, and did the routine thing again, check this and compare that, no changes. Everyone was in the same position, checking little details and waiting, he wanted to talk to them but wouldn't, he wanted to just give them a smile or a thumbs up but he felt he was out there alone, which he was. They were close to fifty yards apart that could have been a mile, Pedro was the only one who was right in the danger zone, he had gone in close to place his little surprise, and three other locations to finalise it, and had stayed in the circle, to back it up when the party started.

He glanced at his watch, it was eleven, one hour to go. He started to wonder what he would do if they decided to have lunch inside today, and that's when he saw the little cloud in the sky and watched it grow. He should have had an alternate plan, what the fuck was he thinking about, now he started to worry all over again, and less than an hour to go, shit!!

It was eleven-fifteen, forty-five minutes to zero and his little cloud was quite big, not blocking the sun yet, but could within the hour. What the fuck if he didn't activate the laser, it was all off for the day, right!

Ten to zero, he brought the snipe into line, dropped the short tripod and slid it forward and bedded it into place, slowly moved his weeds around so none were obstructing his target zone, he knew the other guys were doing the same thing check, check, check, three rounds in the mag and he slowly eased one into the breach and locked it down, placed his crosshairs on the chair junior would occupy then gave himself some eye relief, he pulled the black hood down and adjusted the eyeholes as it was fairly snug and fitted under his chin, and held in place, wiggled the Kevlar back into place, adjusted the chin straps, flipped down the visor with the built-in range finder, placed its crosshairs on the target's chair, 115 yards, exactly the same as yesterday. He didn't know what else to expect if it had said 300 he'd have had a conniption and likely called the whole thing off. He folded up the spotter and stowed it in the Bergen, it was kind of empty right now but could haul out anything worth having. Did a complete check again, at a time like this you could start to fidget, not good, not good at all!

You had to stay calm, watch your field of fire, look for any change in the routine, go over your plan of entry, that was simple, once he had unloaded, it was plain rush making, all the noises you had just been avoiding, and if it moved, shoot it, creating lots of confusion among the staff and anyone out there. There had to be someone that was in charge, they either hadn't seen him or he was so laid back he was hard to pick out and the routine was non-changeable.

Not a breath of wind, now he was looking for excuses. For what? Tightened the velcro on his combat gloves, and it could start any time now, if you were watching TV, this would be the time they would throw in a commercial or a little power outage, and when it came back on you had missed all the good stuff.

His cloud was now twice the size and was moving over the sun, it was three minutes to twelve, no maids in sight, shit they are not going to eat outside, he just knew it! Just with that, one came out and stood with her hands on her hips and looked up at the cloud, it was quite dull by then and he was fit to be tied. Now number one, Ma came swirling in and made a gesture as if to say where is the lunch, so the maid went into some long dialog and was pointing at the sky and his cloud.

Ma was having none of it and waved her hands in the air and pointed at the table and he could imagine what she said as the maid went into high gear. Good old girl and he'd said he didn't like her and she played right into his hands. He could have kissed her big painted toenails, grouchy old bag. In the two-day watch he hadn't seen her smile once, not even come close.

Jim could see the maid's face and it was easy to tell she was shouting for help to start the proceedings, meanwhile the number one lady was strutting around, looking herself over and admiring, he could just tell she thought she was still the cat's mew, the heels were high, the dress was quite short and the boobs were all pushed up and she was swinging around like she was a fashion model, pacing up and down, she had to be sixty at least.

Now the rest of the crew were on site and things were moving, it shook me up that they didn't run in to each other, the nanny arrived with Junior and he was walking a little better and mum gave him a peck on the cheek then returned to her pacing. Junior was helped into his chair and dad came through the door with his two-man fat-boy team of guards. He noticed the guard below, the gun slinger had gone to the concrete block building one and unlocked the door and let the white coats out with their helpers and he headed off to the second hut and repeated the procedure, and walked to the house with them. Guess they got lunch as well.

Back on the patio, platters were on the table and everyone had taken their places, they were ten minutes behind schedule, a lifetime. Everyone was in white, how nice, he put the crosshairs on Junior's shirt, right on his heart and allowed himself the quick look around, to make sure all is clear, no obstructions for the team, all clear, check his target, press the laser button and squeeze the trigger. The red dot appeared and right on top of it his 7.62 entered and expanded and exited with a mess of bone fragments and blood. Mum and Dad were both catapulted right into their food, Junior went over backwards and knocked the nanny on her ass, he chambered another round and took out the guard on the right, just as OJ disqualified the one on the left, the deck was cleared, two maids stuck in the door screaming, five dead.

With the racket from the gunfire reverberating off the canyon walls, it seemed to have doubled. Heads were popping out of every orifice on those tin shacks, the white coats stopped and looked around like some of the guards were having a little fun, they turned and headed on towards the house. That is what you call laid back, crazy. You were out in the bush doing up a couple of mil in cocaine, gunfire starts going off around you, and you wrote it off like foolish children, would they ever learn? He couldn't dawdle any more, he had to make the fence first to show the way. OJ and Chuck would follow him after they unloaded their RPGs.

He dragged his shooting stick back and the legs

folded, ahead he was in a crouch and running the twenty five paces to his RPG location, he dropped to his knees and brushed the leaves and grass back, grabbed the first tube, threw the safety and raised it and sight down the tube, USSR jobbies were side mounted.

So all right-handed, no big deal, he flipped the screen out and looked in, it had a green light with a sunburst sight, eight points with a circle in the middle, put your target in the circle and squeeze.

The smoke and sparks as she took off were quite spectacular, no bang, more a whoosh and a smoke trail. It hit the screen and stuck, this was what they did, they then released a charge that burned its way inside, and caused a swirling inside of hot metal and fragments, with detonations that sprayed in all directions, normally inside an armed personnel carrier or a tank. It would set off the magazines of ammo, usually trays of belt-fed ammo running around the inside walls, so it usually used the inside supply of disaster to cause more disaster, quite successfully.

That is why he hated those death traps. All those wheeled rigs and tracked outfits were targets, not wrong, they had their place but not with him inside, he just didn't like them, he was Infantry through and through, maybe he was slow or something. There was nothing like a fast advance across the terrain with a bunch of infantry riding on a tank, till you hit the first mine then you started counting parts. Not funny.

The building he had struck with his RPG produced a loud pop, a short pause and the explosion was mind boggling and deafening, pieces of tin from the roof and blocks from the walls were sent in all directions, just at this happiness the second building went in the same direction, got that, OJ was right on top of him.

He'd dropped the first tube and grabbed the second and he repeated the maneuver with the first tin hut, just a little further, all pre-sighted, all he did was flip the screen out and squeezed more smoke and fire, there was a whoosh and a boom behind him as Chuck took out the front door of the main home, that oak must have cost ten grand, now kindling if you could find a piece bigger than six inches long, he would complain to the manufacturer.

He just started to hear it, the steady whoosh and beat of rotors getting louder and louder, it was like three gunships all coming out of the jungle at once, then the Tannoy system started up in a good Panamanian-Spanish and this was loud, over and through the choppers and the voice was telling everyone to evacuate to the south, back to their villages, anyone caught in the immediate vicinity will be shot as Cartel members without quarter.

And this was repeated, to say pandemonium would be under-estimating it mildly. There were blue shirts running in all directions, those tin huts were all ablaze and survivors inside were screaming to get out, not much left, the walls were all blown out and nothing but the framework left, fire everywhere, two flash bangs went off and he could feel the ground quiver under him, smoke was in the air and drifting around and doing a great job with all the fire, and their added smoke made it pretty thick and getting worse.

He was so impressed he had to stop to listen. Just below him there was a huddle of maids still in uniform, with their skirts pulled up and running so fast he could almost see their asses. It's something women can do, run for their lives and scream their lungs out at the same time. He guessed it was called multi-tasking, right? He decided to think on that one later, maybe ask Maria and get his ass kicked. Meanwhile they were heading south so fast they would qualify for the Olympics, there was bound to be at least one stroke out of this mad dash, a couple of white shirts were in hot pursuit of the maids, the fast gun was running with one hand holding on to his hat, the other holding his gun deep in its holster, not thinking of pulling it, he might get shot as a bad guy.

That concrete building must have had some pretty bad stuff inside, there was nothing left, blown to the ground. He fired his second into the tin shed and got fire in return, it was burning good, his final and last RPG was for the large propane tank across the gorge, he lined up at the left end that was closest to the house, that was where the filling attachments and gauges, some small twenty-pounders, were lying around, all would help. This would have to be a good hit as the rocket could ricochet off the heavy steel of the tank, as it was all round and cylindrical he hit it reasonably square on and all would be AOK.

He picked his spot and dropped it in, a good hit right on the money, his RPG struck right between the gauges and the feeder pipes, this was the most spectacular blow of the day, his grenade stuck to the target and that was all he remembered. The blast was mind-shattering, it tore out all the windows in the south side of the big house leaving jagged holes, the tank ruptured from end to end and came off its rests and must have gone twenty feet into the air and came down and rolled over the edge and fell down into the gorge below, liquid propane everywhere, with fire in all directions, the grass all around him was burning, pieces of propane tanks were stuck to trees embedded in the walls of the house, with a few bodies blown off their feet, dead and smoldering on the ground, they didn't know what had hit them.

From the first shot till now, under five minutes, this was good, no time to organize and total confusion, piled it on. Chuck had taken his shot at the chopper but couldn't tell if a hit, and no time to study the situation, although this was one shot Jim really wanted to know about, they had broken radio silence on the first shot and shouted encouragement to each other and faster, faster, never to let up. He had used his last tube and dropped it, grabbed his AK104 and started the run and slide to the fence half on his ass.

Half in the air, he hit the fence flat out with both feet and it just folded in front of him, his little tabs breaking off and the mesh falling in. Christ, if it hadn't caved he'd have gone through it and come out like French fries, this shit was sharp, not like your usual chain link, he'd never seen this before, maybe a local product. As he ran he had his AK with the butt under his arm and the fire control in the forward position, fully auto, carrying the snipe in his right hand, and his shotgun on his back, as he ran he dropped the snipe at the door.

He had pulled the bolt and had it in his pant pocket and it was banging against his leg, giving him shit. He never stopped up the bank to the house and gave a burst through a window just to keep heads down and got a long burst in reply, their first retaliation, he ripped a grenade off his webbing and threw it through the window and never stopped, through the door the stairs were right in front of him. Chuck skidded in beside him and threw a smoke down the hall to the right, and a burst right after it, they could hear those 7.62s screaming off those marble tiles, OJ wheeled in and took off to the left, following his smoke then a flash bang (concussion grenade, very loud, leaves you totally disorientated and the flash if direct can cause temporary blindness) hence flash bang. They wore ear-pieces that kept out some, but they still had to cover their ears and eyes, or there wasn't much point. Chuck went right, OJ left and Jim took the stairs, three at a time, now Pedro was behind him. He hit the first landing flat on his belly and Pedro at his elbow sprayed and through. He used smoke, Pedro used HE, that'd work, if it didn't take out the floor, they never spoke, he disappeared into the smoke. Jim headed up to the next floor, the last one, three at a time again, he was puffing and losing sweat, it was running into his eyes and stinging like hell.

He hit the landing on his belly and got a good burst over his head, three white shirts, crouching in the hall midway down, he popped the pin on a concussion and counted two then threw it, blasted them with a long burst, couldn't miss, closed in fast and took his pistol and threw kill shots into them.

Right where the bodies were there was a door, he put his boot to it and nearly fell on his ass, it didn't move. He let the AK dangle from his neck sling and pulled that shotgun round, he'd never used this thing before but simple safety, single and full auto, he flicked it to full and pointed to the doorknob and let it fly, and moved it up, it popped a shot every three inches, then right where the hinges were the door fell in pieces around him and he was in nothing, a bedroom, quick check, nil. Dropped an incinerator and left fast, the blast was right behind him, flash and fire, it burnt everything there was, four more doors in his hallway he reached the next door and it burst open in front of him, a maid with a white shirt and he had an M16 coming up, but he walked right into two shells from the shotgun, the maid got one, he stepped over them, same thing, empty, this was a big room, it took a little longer to cover under the bed and all the closets.

He dropped the fire and left, he looked both ways and the smoke and fire were coming from the first room in good style, he made it to the next door and tried the kick again but he was a slow learner, he swung the shotgun into play. This time he placed two in the middle then the locks, hey this one had a steel coat, the pellets went through, thank God or he could have got nailed by his own ricochets. He pulled the AK up and stepped back and fired a long burst emptying a mag before the kick, he changed out mags, just dropping the empty. He kicked that door hard and it partly opened, nothing coming or going in the hallway, he kicked again, there was some smoke from the firing so he didn't see clearly, at first the room was maybe 10 X 11, with no furniture, but not empty, no sir, it was stacked to about 3ft high with currency, fucking Yankee dollars, British pounds and good old Pesos, he wasn't counting but they just won the Lotto.

He yelled into his mouthpiece,

"Headcount and get an all AOK." Reply. "OK, clean up fast and all on the third ASAP," and he was heading for the last door, it was open and nothing inside. He dropped the fire and left, back to the bank. Chuck was trotting down the hall with OJ, and Pedro was in the rear. He stopped them before the door and said:

"We got a problem," and they all looked at him,

"Like what?"

"Like how are we going to carry this," and he stepped aside. No-one said anything, they just stared in awe. Pedro said something in Spanish and crossed himself, OJ and Chuck said in unison,

"Fuck, we just won the Lotto." Jim started to laugh,

"Hey, that was my line," and they were all laughing. This is the kind of shit you see on TV and no-one believes it, money they can't spend because they can't explain where it came from, or so much they can't spend it all, and as he looked around he thought it was the latter, marble floors, gold taps, nothing but the best. He stopped it real fast, they had twenty miles to go.

"OK OJ, drop your Bergen and head down and make sure all is well, the rest of you fill the bags." They each had full webbing and he stripped off the flak jacket and Chuck followed suit. Jim had one double mag left for the AK104 and discarded the rest. They just took dollars, approximately forty pounds each packed in tight, he filled his ammo pouches and empty water bottle, container pouches, leg pouches on his combat pants and discarded the knee pads that they all came with. They were good to go, he went to a window that was looking out on the courtyard and all the devastation below them, there was fire everywhere, nothing was untouched and no-one was around, all was quiet except the burning and popping and snapping of the fire. He looked in the direction of the strip and saw the small planes burning, but couldn't see the chopper, but he had a feeling and Chuck says he didn't get it. He just knew. Well no point in worrying about it now, let's go, he tossed an incinerator in with what was left, which was most of it and he headed off down the hallway to the stairs, black smoke was everywhere and fire leaping out of doorways.

OJ was off to one side in a crouch behind some crates. They trotted past, he stopped and help him on with his Bergen and they headed out after the other lads. Only one way to go, the same trail they came in on. Pedro took the lead and they followed with a twenty yard spacing. They went about a mile and stopped at a crevice they passed on the way in.

They dumped all the excess gear, sniper Dragunovs worth about $3000 each, Jim's shotgun another two thou, the earpiece headsets unclipped from the Kevlar lids, those they kept and the lids were dropped in a crack with the shotgun and snipers. He beat the shit out of that shotgun and removed the bolts from the snipers and threw them in the opposite direction, they were clean and light, except the packs, they came in with close to eighty pounds and they were leaving with forty, which they hadn't planned on and all uphill, they had just dumped about $20,000 each, the kind of thing you don't think about when some else is paying for it, they called it collateral damage.

They were carrying AK104s and Makarov 9 mils in shoulder holsters that were as light as they could get, so Jim gave the word.

"Move out Pedro and don't spare the horses," and that little fucking Mex went up the trail like his ass was on fire. They ran for fifteen, walked for five, minutes that is, did three sets of that, stop for five, then repeat the system. They came to the spot where they got their first view of the retreat and looked back down. There was some action going on down there, couldn't see much, just little dots running around, but what they did see was that chopper sitting on the pad, all intact. There was a column of about eight dots heading up their back trail.

Chuck gave Jim a nod and he OK'd it, they moved out and Chuck still had two HE grenades so he stayed and set up some surprises, maybe something that might make them think twice before going on. Maybe! They all likely knew what was in that room and they burnt what was left, and they knew they were a small contingent and not their local DEA and they didn't leave empty-handed, so they wanted a piece.

Which they might have got, but it wouldn't come free, that he could guarantee. They might have made the mistake of thinking they were a gang of locals trying to make a fast withdrawal from the local Martinez bank or a rival drug lord moving up, those would both be bad assumptions, real bad. They went to kill and this was their bonus money and they would not give it up easy, and they would kill a few more to prove it. Shit he'd already spent some of it, he could see that baler going around the field already and they wanted it back, come and get her boys, this cowboy don't die easy. And just with that, that fucking chopper flew overhead, they all took cover, he didn't think they'd seen them, but they now knew they meant business and now they would be waiting for them at the extraction point. He wasn't so much worried about them as he was about their ride out. If their chopper saw a firefight he might just go before he got hit himself, couldn't blame him for that. It would take them a year to walk out of that jungle, so they'd better be good, or ready to die.

Jim flipped his talkpiece around and brought in Pedro; He got a "sup boss?" He sounded like he was out for a morning walk, not even panting. "Oh that's nice," so he tried to match it, and damn near choked,

"Make it a sunset arrival Pedro, there is going to be a scrap and I like an evening go."

"You got it boss." They never heard anything from them till they had been on the trail for three hours and some. No-one came down to meet them, they were going to set up, make a nice little ambush and just wait, and get them at the top. Like it was going to be easy! That was when they heard the simultaneous blasts, far behind them, those guys were traveling slowly compared to them. Pedro came back on with one mile to extraction point.

The extraction point would be compromised, they knew that, but they were going to flank them a bit, as much as they could and try to make a little surprise out of it, so they tried to move higher into the mountain a bit, it got in to real dirty going, steep side hill and thick, but they kept it up, they would likely have com sets with them so could communicate, but if they could catch them before the rear party came to where they branched off and not get the word out, all the better, there looked like six or eight in the rear party, eight extra bods they didn't need. The thing was, there was nowhere else for them to go, they had them. They knew that, but they weren't going to make it easy for them.

They just might be able to give them a little surprise, they had circled a little and could go no more for the cliffs, so they started in, but before they moved on them Jim got the VHF out and brought in Cable and he sounded all cheery. He filled him in on their predicament, he now sounded all excited, nice guy, and he came back with some shit,

"I'm fifteen out, get to the edge of the clearing, and when you hear me, give me some pink and keep down."

Pedro had crawled ahead and was doing a light recce. They were in good position for an ambush, if they had stayed on the trail, but they still couldn't get at them easy, they slid in on Pedro and he could see their set up, the old dirt dikes they saw on landing the chopper were out in the open, but well back, he wasn't sure what to do, but if he gave the pink smoke it would give their location up and he heard the incoming thump of the rotors and Cable was shouting,

"Smoke, give me smoke, I got to know where you are." Jim cut in, "don't get fucked up for us."

"Give me the smoke and we will see who's getting fucked up."

Fuck it, he pulled the pin from the canister and threw it out, there was immediate pink smoke right in front of their location, great clouds gently blowing back on them, this was all wrong, now it was drawing fire, good fire, they had more than M16s, maybe a Browning 50, this stuff was big and coming fast, fuck, they couldn't move, they were chewing up what little cover they had, OJ's Bergen took a hit, right on his back, just a little slice, but it threw him on his ass and hundred dollar bills were flying in the air, there went his pocket money.

At least before the smoke they didn't know where they were, it didn't matter with that chopper, they could just keep on moving ahead until they eventually got them whittled down, they couldn't carry any more so if one guy got hit they would have to leave his load, they'd no food, two mags a piece, that's not much, their water was nearly all gone, they had sipped on the climb but still it wasn't going to last for more than a day, there were at least six or eight, judging by the firepower, the chopper on the deck could haul eight easy.

Then it all changed, that big black bird came up from the opposite end of that mountain top, all Jim could see at first was the rotors, then the cockpit and it just hung there, he could barely see his head.

He was sizing up the situation, he thought he was getting ready to leave, but no it started to rise, with a chopper you watch the rotors and when the tips start to lift on the outside, it is rising, then it came over the top three feet off the ground, no ordinary bird.

A Sikorsky uh60 Blackhawk, this bird had four blades, twin engines and could skim the ground at over 200mph.

Jim was looking into the setting sun and all he could see was the outline and it looked good, then the twin Gatlin guns dropped into place, just like that. It started to come in fast, building up speed, those boys were taking notice now and some were diverting their fire to the chopper, he tipped his nose up and started landscaping the terrain around about one hundred feet out from his nose, and it came in so fast that dirt was rising five feet in the air, and it just ran right into them and chopped the shit out of them. There were white shirts diving in all directions, some didn't make it, all of a sudden the tables were turned, shit is flying in all directions, bushes, shrubs, and small trees were all coming down. Fire from all this was catching.

Jim started pumping shells in to the runners, one down and one squealer, nothing like a good squealer to fuck up morale, maybe a knee or gut shot, not nice, three left with the squealer, they were kissing dirt and trying to disappear into it. The other chopper started to rise, they hadn't taken any notice of it but it was going to try to make a run for it, that old hawk just spun around and sent two heat seekers across that table top, approximately a hundred yards, give or take some, and he tore that chopper a brand new asshole; it just disintegrated, pilot and all.

The ball of fire was pretty special, Jim was fucking near crying it was so damned right, their location started to return fire, they opened up to try and create some cover for Cable, not necessary, the son-of-a-bitch dropped a six pack of tubes out and started flying them in on three-second intervals, the smoke was flying, the dirt was dropping on them and it felt like a fucking war zone.

The outside speaker system started to crackle, then it gave a whip-whip! That was to get your attention, then Cable came on.

"You guys stop admiring the fucking view and get your asses out here so we can go home."

They all rose without another word and ran like hell for that chopper, it was just hanging three feet off the deck and gently swaying back and forward with each grenade it punched out, man they didn't make movies this good, Stallone would be on the edge of his seat. Jim ran last and just feet before they reached the door he swung it broadside so they were looking at the boarding door and the skid was 2-3 feet off the deck. He turned and emptied his last mag in their direction, and hit that skid full tilt and that mother's son just banked that bird hard and dropped it over the edge of that cliff so fast and spun it around facing north, and they were gone. They were so tipped up he thought he was going to go right through. They were all on the floor and hanging on to each other and anything that was protruding. He was looking at the tree tops about three hundred feet below wondering if he fell out would they hold him. He lay flat on his belly and held on and he just levelled it off and Jim started laughing and laughing and so did everyone else, Cable was wooing, whooping.

"Wow man, wasn't that just right on man. Just right on! Fuck, I'm good man! Oh you guys are going to get a little adjustment on your bill for the extra firepower, I can't afford that on mine. I just get flying money."

"Don't you worry about the bill, bud" and they all laughed some more.

"Why? You guys get some good scran?"

"Well you might say that, just a little, might even be a buck in it for you."

"Hey that sounds great, could use an extra meal once in a while. Them other jockeys I haul for give shit, never even talk, they can sit back there for two hours and never say a word, not even a thank you."

"You been hanging out with the wrong crowd, my friend."

"You got that right, I haven't had so much fun since I left Afghanistan, I'm glad I got the call to tote you guys, this has been a blast, I didn't realise how much I missed it. Hey your duffel bag is in the back hanging in the cadge."

"Thanks." The cadge is a net pouch you would throw anything you didn't want to fall out, if you were maneuvering with the doors open, like escape and evasion, just what they came through. Guys like Cable practised those maneuvers, they were vital to any pick-up crew once you have picked up your people, get out of vision and range as fast as possible, in the air you're still the target, and don't forget it. The guy that thinks he is invincible is dead and there are lots of them with no story to tell! We had lucked out with a guy like Cable, some jockeys would have run the minute they saw fire or come in too fast and not got low enough, and you got to climb in, too slow, they would be flopping around, their rotors would come so low you couldn't get near them and you would draw fire and someone was going down, easy targets, guys trying to climb into a chopper that is five feet off the ground and swinging around, so Cable was AOK.

They were skimming through the jungle at a ridiculous speed, so low that some kid could have hit them with a rock, but they were out and no pursuit, they had nothing to follow with, whoever was left that was, the way that cannon tore up those dirt banks, then the RPGs man, you might be able to find enough parts to rebuild one or two of them, kind of mix and match.

OJ reached behind and pulled out the bag and started pulling out those clothes they had stashed, in the bag they each had a bundle, just jeans and T-shirts, and they started stripping off and climbing into their bundles. Jim liked cowboy boots, no laces just tug them on and great for a concealed weapon. Cable came on and said any hardware to get rid of, this is the place to do it, they were over a gorge with no bottom, they could see just raging water going in and they tossed their AK104s and those black pants and shirts, they had to stash their spare cash in the duffel. He had stuffed every pouch or water bottle container full of bundles of hundred dollar bills, there were tens and twenties and fifties, they left them all and only took the hundreds. OJ put his Bergen right inside his duffel and zipped it up, he couldn't have lost more than a couple of grand.

"Hey, you want pocket change, I'll get it for you. It's funny, a hundred dollar bill weighs no more than a five, so which do you want?" They threw all the handgun harnesses out as well and Jim stuck his in his boot top and pulled his jeans over it. The boys stuck theirs in the back and their T-shirts over them. Then they slid into the net seats, slid the doors closed and the noise stopped, that's when he told the guys about Cable's little predicament, that he couldn't afford to buy the chopper. Chuck said:

"You want to buy it for him?"

"Well we could buy it and make him an equal partner, we're not just going to drop one point five on him, that would be too easy, but he could be handy in the future."

"Good point" OJ said and all the guys nodded their approval, Pedro nodded and said:

"That hombre can fly me any time."

Jim dumped out the holdall again and started counting the bundles back in to the bag, there was one point seven which just blew them away.

They never counted when filling the kit bags, they just stuffed them full, then their pants and bottle bags, not thinking how much they had. Fill them and flee, that was kind of how it went. They didn't know how much retaliation they would have. As it turned out, if it wasn't for Cable they would have been in a lot of shit.

But one thing they all knew, they all had a lot more than was in that bag sitting on the floor, which made them feel kind of good. Cable came on the talker and said:

"We are in Costa Rica, just crossed the border not five minutes ago, we will be landing on a jungle strip out of Limon, we are moving fast. When I land, grab your gear and let's unload, there will be an old DC waiting for us and we are gone. I will come back and strip all the toys off the ship later, and move it back to its owner, I'm going to miss this thing, but I might get to fly it again, who knows? The DC is registered in Mexico so no problem once we get there, but until then it's low flying, and I'm going to fly you right to that fancy strip in Pedro's backyard and from there you are on your own."

"You are going to land in my back yard? Hey Cable, you haven't seen my strip."

"Yeah I took a detour over it yesterday, on a run to LA. It's a snap." Then Chuck said:

"Don't let Pedro think it's a snap, the next thing he'll start to thinking it's LAX and want to go commercial." This brought a chuckle from the rest of them. That's when Jim thought, I should learn to fly and he said it, Pedro said:

"Yeah compadre, me too, I got a strip so I should learn to fly, Chuck is always telling me how easy it is. That's when Cable came on and said he would give lessons cheap, Pedro shook his head,

"No way compadre, it is flying lessons I want, not suicide lessons, remember we have flown with you."

"Oh damn, so you have" and there is another round of laughter "What about you Jim?"

"Sorry I think I'll just stick to the tractor."

"A tractor? You as well! Pedro has one, I saw it yesterday. What have I got here, a bunch of fucking farmers with guns?"

"Yup, a country boy can survive."

"Wow this is some dangerous trip for me, I'm a city boy."

That's when Chuck and OJ got into the picture, Chuck said,

"Don't sweat it Cable, these country hicks get vertigo with bright lights, but I'm with you right OJ?"

"You got it man, loud music and loose women, nothing like it to get your morale up and your cholesterol down."

"Shit man, it sounds like farmers and lawyers. What did I do wrong?"

"Not a thing man, not a thing."

Chuck said "I guess I'm just hanging out with the right people."

"Now that's talking" Jim said.

"OK guys, five to LZ, I got a special pad I got to land on, it's just a big dolly, but it has wheels and they can drag it inside the hangar till I get back, so I can strip it and hose off the black, it's just water colour, you spray it on, you spray it off. Jim looked at Chuck and said:

"Isn't modern technology just wonderful, what will they think of next?"

Cable came on the talker and was using perfect Spanish and talking to the ground, it came back loud and clear, but just a jabber to Jim.

"You get that Pedro?"

"Not a goddam word, was that Spanish?" he asked.

"Hey, we are in Costa Rica, it's all different here"

"OK, when I touch down, bail and head for the DC, I'll be right there, it should be running."

It was pitch black, but they came in fast and started to wobble about, then there was a little drop and they were on the dolly, the rotors were still spinning but the door was open and they were gone. Jim headed straight for the DC, he was carrying both bags, his and the holdall for Cable, there was a little drop down door with steps on it, they did a lot of jumps from these old things, they had two doors with a trap on the floor you could unload fast and nothing had changed, all side jump seats, just nets that you pulled over yourself so you could sleep and not fall out, he dumped the bags into one and hooked them in, then himself.

Cable was right behind them and the next thing was the rpm went way up and the old bird started to move, he didn't have to ask what they had been using this thing for, the smell of Mary Jane was intoxicating, Pedro was watching Jim and he just smiled.

"I feel like I'm home already" and he chuckled. No taxi time, no talk, just wheeled it around and into the wind and full rpm and release, shit they were airborne and low, like he said.

"OK boys and girls, its ZE time but it's going to be bumpy so do the best you can, we will be in Mexico by first light and then Pedro Commercial, if I don't get shot down by a Mex Mig and I'm going to be bagged, you got a spare bunk for a compadre Pedro, just for a few hours?"

"Hey amigo, you get me home to my Maria I will give you a sweet and good woman as well."

"Hey Chuck, you ever get offered a woman?" Jim asked.

"No way, that's favoritism."

"No I'm just scared of his flying and I will do anything to get home safe."

All this banter and fast talk was just a come-down, the adrenalin was all dried up and it didn't feel so good, almost nauseous, but that was just him so he hung himself forward into the net with his bag between his legs and fell into the deep sleep that only exhaustion can give.

It was over, all they had to do was get the money into a Mexican bank and it was done, some folks tell you not to deal with Mexican banks as they play games. Not true, if you have enough cash they take interest and if you want to invest in their country, here comes the red carpet. He just wanted to bank it, get a visa and let them pay the bills, there was no interest for gringos without all kind of paper work, he didn't need interest. He was going to buy something down there on the beach, but not just now, all he could think of was his mountain home and solitude for at least a week.

At Pedro's he would drop a mail to the Commander and give him the success story, he could take the last 500 grand and pay the bills, take his cut and give the rest back to the lady, that sounds OK. She would never get over her daughter, they hurt them for her, but they didn't take away the pain, just punished them some. He didn't come to till he felt the bounce at Pedro's International, it was the best sight Jim had seen in a while. His old pick-up was in the yard waiting, they all bailed out and went in different directions to their little spots, the guest cabins were still empty, Cable spun that old tub around and shut it off and it chugged to a standstill and he wandered out looking around. Jim gave him a wave and he followed.

He went to the cabin he had used on departure and it was open, he threw his gear on the first sack inside the door and pointed to the adjoining room and flicked on the lights. Cable just blinked some, Jim turned on the shower and said "You're first bud," and he just nodded.

THE PUNISHER

That guy was all in on his feet, they had landed and fuelled up and taken off again and he said OJ, Chuck and Jim never opened their eyes till the first bump at Pedro's. Now they hit the first hot water since they left a week ago and it felt good. He dried off and fell on that sack, he was out before he hit the pillow.

Then wide awake with someone beating the shit out of the iron triangle Pedro had hanging off the porch. He glanced at his watch and it was 2100, no-one had ever got to sleep that late on this ranch before. He staggered to the shower again and did a lukewarm one, just to waken up, then got dressed and beat the door to Cable's and stuck his head in and he was round-eyed, looking at him.

"What the hell was that noise?"

"That my friend was the cook saying it was time to refuel, so shake a leg and let's chow up in this place, it is good eating let me tell you." And he left him to get it done and wandered over for his first coffee.

Just the best, and a smoke that wasn't flattened out and bent in the middle, and all covered with the yellow stain that sweat puts on them, or maybe a little crack that you don't see and it leaves you sucking your brains out.

Man if you kept life simple it sure was good, just the simple things could give you so much pleasure. He had on a clean T-shirt, his old jeans that Maria had washed and his well-worn shit-kicking cowboy boots. Maria brought him this big steaming cup of Java and gave him a hug, then whispered into his ear,

"Thank you for bringing my Pedro back Senor Jim."

"My pleasure."

He thought that they all brought each other back, one way or the other, that Cable deserved a big hand for the part he played.

They were all there, just sipping and yacking, waiting for the Cable guy to show. They had decided to give him his cut after they ate, then they had to go to town with Pedro and do some banking. Cable came out stuffing his shirt inside his jeans. Maria and the kids were busy hauling out the food and she stopped and came to Cable and gave him a hug in front of everyone and thanked him for bringing her boys home safe, this threw him for a loop and he was stammering and everything, and nodding his head like a chicken, and they were all having a good laugh at his expense. Maria came to the rescue and told everyone to sit and eat before it got cold, and they did, all making fools of themselves and over-eating, which is understandable after the diet they just had for a week, oatmeal blocks were all right and suffice, but a week was long enough and water with chlorine pills, it kind of gets to you after a while, so they enjoyed their food and showed it.

They were all wrapped up and smoking and sipping coffee when Jim asked Cable what was up for him after this.

"Well, I've got to get back and strip that chopper and see if I can find another run from those guys. Got to make a living man."

Jim said, "Say, how about we take you on as a partner with us?"

"Oh yeah, doing what? All I know is flying, I'm not much good at that ground stuff you guys do."

"Well we were thinking on buying a chopper, but none of us have the smarts to fly it, so we thought maybe you would like the job."

"You got one in mind? I'd better tell you, those things cost a real bucket of money, see that one we just came out in, it is not new, but it is on the block for 1.5 mil and that is a steal, so you better really think that thing out. Hey guys, I really appreciate the offer but I'm trying to get into something legit and maybe stretch my life expectancy a few more years. I just can't go on being lucky, you know what I mean?"

"Well that is just what we were thinking. Something legal, no bending the law, well maybe on the odd occasion, if it was really necessary, you know what I mean" and there was a chuckle around the table.

"Well guys, that sounds great, I've got all kinds of work I could get if I had my own chopper. But unfortunately no tooth fairy and I'm all out of silver spoons."

Jim nodded to Chuck and he threw him the bag and said,

"This group of fairies ain't so good looking but we got the goods." Chuck one-handed the bag into the air and Cable caught it, or he was going off the bench.

"What's this then?"

"Take a look and see," and he dropped the holdall on the table and unzipped it and stuffed his hands inside, and they could see a frown coming over his face, he knew what it felt like but wouldn't let his brain believe it, and he pulled out two handfuls of cash, all hundred dollar bills.

"What the fuck is this?" and his eyes were huge with

disbelief, maybe thinking they were going to take it back from him.

"Well Cable, that is our buy-in money. That chopper is 1.5, in the bag is 1.7 and we will be silent partners in that chopper, if you will have us, that is."

He just looked around the table and had this stupid grin like he still didn't believe it was happening to him, and a tear started to roll down his cheek. Pedro said "Is that little tear a yes or a no?"

He slowly shook his head and covered his face with his hands and they waited maybe a minute. He took down his hands and looked around the table, then said "When do we start?"

They all clapped and gave him a cheer, it was good for them all. He got fifty percent of the take and they got the rest and no bills to pay, the chopper was clear title.

He just didn't know what he had bought into yet, but Jim didn't think he would mind. He thought he was the kind of guy that needed a little fire once in a while, just to see if all the dots were in the right place. And he was sure the Commander hadn't written him off, something else would pop up, it always did. He just wished he would leave the hunting season out and when the fish are biting, of course they bit a lot on his lake.

Oh some questions would arise, but they would fix that, Pedro's uncle was the President of the Imperial Bank of Mexico and with a little palm greasing all would be taken care of, it had before and would again. What Jim didn't know was that one million dollars US in one hundred dollar bills weighed twenty two lbs. or 10 kg, if you piled it four-wide and twelve inches high that was one mil, their packs held almost right on, two mil each, not counting their pockets and ammo pouches, and weighed forty-four lbs each pack. That shook them up real bad, they had eight mil between them.

Pedro thought he'd better make a casual visit to his uncle, to see if he could, or would handle it. This would take another couple of days, Cable was free to go and buy their chopper and he left that afternoon and said he was flying high and still on the ground. There was a lot of hand-shaking and back-slapping before he took off. And as they stood and watched him soar into the air, they all knew if he hadn't stuck his neck in the noose, they wouldn't have been around today, just critter feed on a hill in Panama. Pedro said for them to hang loose till he got back, and it might not be for a couple of days, so they lay around and drank their pal's beer and spent money in their heads, and dreamed of good things. Good places and punishments made, and well deserved.

And just when the next one would come.

PUNISHER #2

THE TEMPERATURE IS -35 CELSIUS. I HAVE APPROXIMATELY five point eight hours of daylight, if you can call it that. First light is in one hours' time making it around eight forty five, there is a light snowfall keeping it from dropping any further, thank the Lord for small mercies. My immediate location is eight hundred point five meters from an all-male prison. Situated approximately twenty kilometres from the city of Anadyr, as the crow flies, thought I'd throw that in, as there is no road. Only access is by airbus, prisoners are flown into this location with the good chance of never leaving it alive, I say that as it is only long haul guys that make it to this location, all supplies come on a scheduled trip every Friday, weather permitting. Guards rotate on a six week in and a three week out. The warden stays all the time, by choice!

The reason I'm here? I'm fifteen kilometers from the Baring Strait, downhill all the way, I can see the fog where the sea ice ends, you have around three clicks of ice at this time, it will increase till January or February. In the middle of the straits are the islands of Big Diomede and little Diomede, Big Diomede belongs to Russia, Little Diomede belongs to the US of A, they are situated thirty k apart or thereabouts, that is where Sara says she can see Russia from Alaska, it's one island to the other and they can walk across, when it is frozen, that is, as it does between the islands in midwinter.

Anadyr has eleven point two thousand population, mostly Chukchi or Inuit, the rest Ruskies and they got to be hiding from something or on a scientific mission to hell. The place looks like an Olympic village or the place Russia dumps its off-colour paint no longer required. An apartment can have three colours diagonally across its front, yellow, green and red, no problem, any colour you want, I don't know when it gets to dry, or if it's just frozen on, anyway it's nothing to write home about.

Crews looking for oil or drilling crews taking core samples, all on government payroll, good ones I hope! I'm buried in two hundred centimeters of fresh snow looking down on the prison. I can see part of the center court yard and the warden's quarters in the center of the back wall facing the courtyard, it is on the third floor of a four-floor building. The warden has a built-out patio of plexiglass running on three sides, about one and a half meters high. The patio is two and a half meters deep and all around open on the top, this is where he will perform his callisthenics in the morning, as every morning. Something to inspire the staff and let the inmates see that he has lost it completely. The outside perimeter has a five hundred meter dead zone clear and flat on all fronts, mines and booby traps of various kinds, beyond the five hundred meter zone. To the seven hundred meter zone is saturated with surveillance equipment, not the latest technology but adequate they think, that is why I'm at the eight hundred and five meter mark, outside the blanket area, they feel quite secure and I'm glad they do.

At eight forty five the warden will perform for his staff and inmates. And at eight fifty I will terminate him, as that is why I'm here, and that is what I do, besides other things, I am a mercenary, or a soldier of fortune. And this was a contract I chose to fulfill.

This will hit the street 2015 I hope!

The first novel, 'The Boy the Man' will
have a sequel, it just takes time.